THE NECROMANCER'S APPRENTICE

THE NECROMANCER'S APPRENTICE

BEVERLY TWOMEY

Snowy Wings
PUBLISHING

TURNER, OR

For those who hold onto hope in the midst of unbearable darkness.
May you always remain gentle and kind.

Contents

Chapter One

A graveyard is often filled with great sorrow, loss, and memory. But for the darkly inclined magic practitioner, it is the place where our studies begin.

  - The Dying Art of Necromancy, *Author Unknown*

* * *

It always rained at funerals in Yoricsgrave. Sometimes the rain came with a tremendous thunderstorm with lightning strikes that kept most of the grieving in their homes. Other times, it was a light rain, dappled with sunlight. But today, the rain was a miserable drizzle.

The overcast sky mimicked the soggy gray mourning garb of the villagers as they gathered in front of the stone church in the center of the graveyard.

Georgie and his father, the Blacksmith, were towards the end of the procession. They made a unique pair, standing at the edge of a funeral. The Blacksmith was tall, broad-shouldered and stern, as if the iron he worked with had fused into his very spine. Years of working the forge had left his arms toned and strong. His black hair lay slicked back from the rain, but the water drizzled down the graying beard on his face.

The twelve-year-old Georgie was reaching the stage where he was too old to be babied and yet too young to be considered an adult. He was an awkward tangle of lengthening limbs the size of sapling trees. With bright-red hair and even brighter green eyes, the boy looked very different from his father.

Neither had known the deceased personally, but with a village as small as Yoricsgrave, you at least knew of a person. Thus, they were here to pay their respects.

Georgie itched underneath his oversized oilskin. He couldn't see with the hood over his eyes, so he'd gone without it. Now, he regretted such a choice as the cold rain had nowhere else to go but down his back.

Georgie looked around over the damp headstones of the graveyard. "Where's Ellory?"

"Quiet, Georgie," his father rumbled beside him, the only thunder during this storm. He stared straight ahead with his arms crossed over his broad chest. His father hated funerals.

So why does he always insist that we attend?

Georgie's eyes fell sullenly to his feet, now ankle-deep in mud. There wasn't much you could do at a funeral for someone you hadn't known. He couldn't hear the Priest speaking from this far away. There had been other funerals more celebratory than this, even with the rain. But this? This was a hushed sadness that demanded a whisper. If words were to be spoken at all. But that had never stopped a village gossip.

"Did you hear what happened?" a villager murmured to her companion. "How the Old Woodsman died?"

"I did," her companion replied, speaking out of the side of her mouth. "Said they found him at the base of the hills to the north."

"It's odd that he should have fallen," said the first. "The Old Woodsman was like a mountain goat. So sure-footed."

"I heard it wasn't the fall that killed him," added another villager. "He'd been wounded. Badly. By some sort of wild animal. Bitten all over and scratched to pieces. He was raving about some sort of 'creature' with his last breath."

The chill down Georgie's spine intensified.

"It's strange," said the first villager. "They found him where the first accident happened. What was that, six years ago? When the Lady Smith—"

The Blacksmith cleared his throat, silencing the chattering villagers.

Ah, thought Georgie. *There it is.*

He often kept watch, staying vigilant should any of the Blacksmith's six-year-old sorrow come back to haunt him. It would start slowly at first, but the Blacksmith's rumbling was one of the first signs. However, there would be no reaching his father here.

Georgie tugged at his father's sleeve. "I'm going to go see Mum."

The Blacksmith responded with a silent nod as Georgie slipped away.

Georgie stooped down every few steps, gathering a handful of drooping clover flowers as he went. The graveyard lay in a small valley surrounded by trees. Most preferred to be buried closer to the church, forever resting amongst generations of family members. But there were a few graves that dotted the hillsides, lingering closer to the trees.

At the base of a weeping willow tree sat a single gravestone, more worn than he'd remembered. In his mind, the stone was always bright marble, as it had been on the day of another funeral six years ago. The rain had dulled the engraving, but even as Georgie brushed the water aside, he knew it by heart.

Here lies Adelaide Smith. Beloved Wife, Mother, and Sister.

Forever at Peace in Rest Undisturbed.

"Hi, Mum," he said.

Georgie's mum was more of this silent headstone than a person. He'd been very young when she'd passed, so Georgie relied on others to fill in the gaps of his memory.

She'd been an incredibly bright woman, his teachers had told him, quick-witted and clever with a wide smile. Her sister, his Aunt Elisa, had said his mother had been beautiful and kind. Her patience had been never-ending. Even as much as she or his own father had tested it.

Georgie knew her by what his father didn't say. Rarely did he speak of her, but Georgie saw the sadness in his father's eyes. He knew that there was a photograph kept beside the Blacksmith's bed. The picture was of a smiling woman held in the arms of her husband, untouched by grief.

Most people had mothers. Georgie couldn't help but notice the absence of his.

But how do you miss something that you never knew?

He didn't dare ask anyone this question, even as it lingered, growing stronger and stronger each year after her passing. He certainly couldn't speak of it to his father and dare diminish his father's heartbreak with something that felt so profane.

Perhaps if he knew her better, he would understand the Blacksmith's grief. Perhaps then he would know how to say his own goodbyes.

"There you are!" a cheerful voice called out, startling Georgie out of his reverie.

Ellory, his cousin, climbed up the hill behind him. Ellory stuck out by sheer virtue of her enthusiasm. Pinned to her gray oilskin, a half dozen dandelions danced across the collar. Her oversized hat, tied at her chin, was dripping with water as if it were a raincloud itself. Her bright-red cheeks were held up by a smile. Only Ellory could smile like that in a graveyard.

"I've been looking all over for you. The service is nearly over."

Georgie cast a glance back at his mother's gravestone. As if the marker would have any objection to him going away. Sometimes he wished it would. But the stone lay silent as he followed Ellory down the hill.

The ten-year-old girl held a weathered notebook up to her face, trying to shield it from the rain with her hat brim as she scribbled madly into it.

"What are you doing?" asked Georgie.

"Note-taking," she said. "I was asking around to see if everyone agreed with how the Old Woodsman died."

"Agreed? What's there to disagree about? He's dead."

"I'm not debating that," she said pointedly, but she was still smiling. "I'm more interested in *how*."

Ah. It was another one of Ellory's 'investigations.' The girl loved to find a mystery in everything. Sometimes it was as simple as 'How did the ants make it into the sugar bowl again?' and other times it was larger questions such as 'What are the geological implications of the many valleys in Yoricsgrave?' She took great pride in baffling her teachers and asking inappropriate questions, much to her mother's despair.

"What sort of creature do you think could have killed the Old Woodsman?" said Ellory. "The man's entire house was filled with taxidermy creatures. He told me he'd even fought off a centaur before!"

"Animals are dangerous," said Georgie with a shrug, a phrase his father had used as a mantra for the past six years.

"But not for Oldman Woodsman!" Ellory exclaimed. "He couldn't have gotten to be so old otherwise." She shut her notebook with a satisfied snap while tapping her pencil to her chin. "There's a mystery here. I know it."

They made their way back down the hill, the ground beneath their feet squelching in muddy protest. The service must have concluded, as the crowd dispersed away from the chapel. But Ellory wasn't going around or taking him back to the Blacksmith.

"Wait a minute," said Georgie. "Where are we going?"

Ellory grinned. "We're going to see the last rites." She slipped through the crowd as easily as if she were a breeze. Georgie bumped and tripped his way behind her, murmuring apologies as they emerged at the front.

The Priest closed his tome with a wet smack, folding it underneath his arm before returning inside the chapel. Ellory snuck around the building to the opposite side, leaning out as much as she dared from behind the corner to see the sodden coffin of Oldman Woodsman, now accompanied only by the gravedigger.

Georgie peeked over Ellory's shoulder, poking her lightly in the side. "We need to get back."

Ellory shooed his hand away and pointed.

The shadows of the chapel stepped away as a tall figure, dressed in drenched black, emerged. This person wore a cloak instead of an oilskin, making the fabric cling to the lanky body beneath it. The hood was drawn, so Georgie couldn't see their face.

The shadow slunk towards the coffin of the deceased. A thin

bone-white hand appeared from beneath the cloak, holding a long piece of white chalk.

The figure drew across the coffin, wiping off the puddles of water as they did so. With a mix of alchemical circles, swirls of a language Georgie didn't understand, and a final flourish, the figure seemed satisfied. Another hand emerged from the cloak to rest beside the other as the figure pressed down upon the coffin lid.

By now, the villagers were several yards away. The only one who seemed aware was the gravedigger, who looked as pale as death himself. He shifted nervously in the mud, his hands squeaking around the hilt of the shovel as the figure muttered under their breath. Georgie thought it might be a prayer until the chalk glowed.

It was slow at first, radiating out from the bone-white hands as if there were some semblance of warmth to them. The glow was soft before becoming brighter and brighter in a vibrant blue.

The hair on Georgie's arms stood on end. There was a pressure building on his ears and chest. Ellory didn't seem to notice. Her eyes were solely locked on to the figure while her pencil flew across the page of her notebook with a will of its own. The damp strands of her hair were slowly rising in the air, being pulled towards whatever this was.

Crack!

The sound echoed across the graveyard, as sharp and sudden as a lightning strike. The blue glow of the chalk faded, dripping down the edges of the coffin and onto the ground below.

Something had been severed, shut and locked away. Forever.

The figure stood straight, removing their hands from the coffin and returning them to the shadows of their cloak.

Without a word to anyone, the figure walked away, disappearing into the gray as if they'd never been there at all.

"Who was that?" asked Georgie.

Ellory gave a satisfied smile. "That was the Necromancer."

Chapter Two

There are a number of skills required to study magic. A strong mind, a heart filled with hope, and a stubbornness that even the most cantankerous of mules cannot muster. This is why many a magic practitioner begins their tutelage when they are children, for who else but a child has all of these in abundance?
 - The Dying Art of Necromancy, *Author Unknown*

* * *

The next day, the sun returned. The warmth of late summer quickly brought life back to the village of Yoricsgrave, nestled deep within the valley. It wasn't the largest of settlements by any means, but it had access to the Road, and by that means alone, it was useful. Bright-blue skies greeted the lazy tendrils of wood smoke from the chimneys, while the cool mountain breeze swept them away as if brushing hair from a child's face, fond and gentle.

Georgie's home lay on the eastern side of the village. It was a large two-story house with wide glass windows, hand-carved decorative trim on all sides, and roof tiles of ruby red. It had been an impressive wedding present from a man who'd thought his wife would be around long enough to fill it with life, laughter, and half a dozen children.

Instead, it was just Georgie and his father.

The house lay quiet as Georgie stirred awake. He'd fallen asleep in his seat by the window again, his abandoned book still perched on top of his chest. It was a comfortable place, covered in cushions, blankets and with an ever-present pile of used teacups on the floor beside it.

Georgie stretched with a yawn and rolled out of his nest to get dressed. He tugged on a simple homespun shirt of dark green and rough brown trousers that were patched at the knees. Before he went downstairs, he gathered up the teacups, spoons, and other crumb-covered dishes to bring with him. He could already hear his aunt singing in the kitchen below.

Georgie remembered the days before Aunt Elisa had swooped in.

The large house had suffered during the early years of Adelaide's absence. The Blacksmith was a working man. He wasn't untidy, but it wasn't easy raising a small child, keeping a home, and running a business. The fires of the forge couldn't go out if they were to survive.

But after a few difficult months, Aunt Elisa had come to visit.

Georgie had broken his collarbone. He'd been trying to reach an impossibly dusty corner on the stairs when he'd fallen, tumbling down with a loud enough crash that the Blacksmith had run in from the forge. Georgie would heal well enough, but it meant that his arm had been kept safely tucked away in a small sling for several months. He remembered how hot his ears had burned when his aunt had seen the house for the first time.

"Alistair! How long have you been living like this?" She'd surveyed the cobwebs and the mound of dirty dishes, tapping at the stale bread on the counter.

"It's fine," grumbled the Blacksmith.

"It is most certainly not! If Adelaide were here—"

"But she's not," the Blacksmith had said sharply.

Aunt Elisa had wilted, the teasing smile fading from her lips. "I know, Alistair. I know."

The Blacksmith had turned his back towards her, tackling the dishes with the same brutal strength he used at the forge. Until Aunt Elisa had slipped beside him, rolling up her sleeves. "They're porcelain dishes, not steel," she'd said gently. "You'll break every dish in the house at this rate. Let me help."

In that quiet moment, something had been decided, and ever since then, Aunt Elisa had been a ray of sunshine, one that brushed away the gloom of the empty house with a cheerful smile, a persistent dust cloth, and tea always at the ready.

Currently, Aunt Elisa was up to her elbows in soapsuds as she washed dishes at the large sink. Georgie tried hard to find similarities between the woman in his kitchen and the picture on the mantel. Aunt Elisa often boasted that she was taller than her older sister, Adelaide, had been. But her hair was a deeper auburn that she kept pulled back in a bun. The curls she did have would often escape throughout the day, framing her face.

Georgie sheepishly added his stack of teacups next to her on the counter.

Aunt Elisa raised an eyebrow, her deep-hazel eyes glittering with amusement. "Is that all of them?"

Slowly, Georgie reached into his pocket and gave her a pile of teaspoons as well.

His aunt laughed, plucking the spoons from his hand and leaving a dab of soap on his nose. "Here I thought they were running away with the dishes."

Georgie grinned, rubbing away the soap. "Can I help with anything?"

"Of course," she said, wiping her hands on her apron. She went to the stove, where an old iron kettle sat, gently whistling. She poured a generous cup before placing it on a tray with a slice of bread and soft cheese.

"Take this out to your father, will you? He's been at the forge since I arrived this morning."

Like a cloud covering the sun, Georgie felt a familiar shadow fall over him. "Did you talk to him?"

Aunt Elisa shook her head. "No, but you know how your father is. It's easy for him to get caught up in his work."

Georgie knew all too well. He took the tray. "Thank you, Aunt Elisa."

His aunt smiled, soft and warm, just like the picture of his mother on the mantel. "You're welcome, Georgie."

He stepped out into the morning sunshine and headed down the hill towards the south side of the house, following the rhythmic sounds of a hammer hitting metal.

Tink. Tink. Tink.

The Blacksmith's forge was well known in Yoricsgrave. Georgie's great-grandfather had founded it, and each son after him had worked it. His father had taught him a few things, always eager to show Georgie and ever patient when he inevitably messed it up. But Georgie never managed to get the hang of the work. His hands felt too small, his arms too thin to ever gain any of the necessary muscle.

"It's all right, son. Keep to your books," the Blacksmith would say, taking the tools from his hands. "You take after your mother."

Georgie didn't like that he so often reminded his father of the wife he'd lost. Another reason to stay quiet. Another reason for him to mourn. And yet, the similarity alone wasn't enough to solve the problem of his father's grief.

His father's workshop smelled of woodsmoke and rough iron. Georgie's eyes adjusted to the gloom that overshadowed the area, focusing in on the familiar orange glow of the forge, where the Blacksmith was mending a new cauldron. He heated the metal first, turning it skillfully in the flames until it glowed white. The Blacksmith's hammer fell upon the metal with careful precision, with the strength behind his strikes shaping it as easily as if it were clay. Carefully, the Blacksmith took up the metal again, setting it into the pots of water stationed nearby. With a loud hiss, the metal cooled.

His work complete for the moment, Georgie's father turned to him. "Morning, boy."

"Morning, Da," he replied, motioning to the tray in his hands. "Aunt Elisa told me to bring you this."

"Time to eat already?" The Blacksmith's mouth lifted to one side with a smile. "Come. Sit with me."

Georgie took the tray to the small wooden table. He sat on one of the wooden blocks while his father sat on a tall stool on the other side. The Blacksmith took the apple off the tray, removed a small knife from the pocket in his apron, and began cutting it into slices. He gave half to Georgie, keeping half for himself.

The two ate in companionable silence as they gazed out from the forge towards the rest of the town. It was a ritual they'd long perfected over the six years since his mother's death; the

Blacksmith lost in his own thoughts, and his son desperately trying to find him.

"Aunt Elisa said you were already at the forge when she arrived," said Georgie.

The Blacksmith grunted, his gaze still distant. "I was."

"And you didn't eat breakfast," he said, pointing to the untouched bread and cheese on his father's plate.

The Blacksmith looked back to his meal, startled out of his reverie. "Sorry, son. There's been a lot on my mind." He dutifully spread the soft cheese on top of the bread, raised it in salute, and took a bite. "It's good," he said as crumbs dropped onto his beard. "Be sure to send my compliments to Elisa."

Georgie nodded, but the earlier shadow of concern for his father grew. Long work hours, terse silence and isolation, and lack of self-care. He sighed inwardly. It must have been the funeral, the single stone that had begun a rock slide.

The Blacksmith set his hand on top of Georgie's. "Thank you, son. What would I do without you?"

The possibilities, each more worrisome than the last, played through Georgie's mind. He would do whatever it took to prevent each and every one. "You're welcome, Da."

"Hello? Anyone home?" A man's voice broke the gloom.

The Blacksmith wiped his face and stood to greet the newcomer. "Morning, Callum. What brings you in?"

Callum Paddock was the younger Blacksmith of the village. Georgie remembered the rumors of another Blacksmith opening up shop in Yoricsgrave. The village wives had whispered that perhaps the first Blacksmith was going to move away. But Georgie's father didn't bother listening to them. There was more than enough work for the two Blacksmiths. Instead, the Blacksmith had taken Callum under his wing, helping the younger man, who was often eager to impress but less consistent upon delivery.

"A commission, sir. Or at least, one that I can't seem to crack." Callum rubbed at his short, cropped brown hair with one hand while holding out a heavy length of chain with the other. "You know the man who lives out in the foothills? He's commissioned a special length of chain."

The Blacksmith took the drooping metal from Callum's hand, inspecting it. "Looks strong enough to me. You haven't needed help with chain work for years now."

"It's not the chain work that's the problem," Callum explained. "It's the magic he wants inscribed into it." He reached into his apron pocket, pulling out a handful of paper. "I've never seen any runes like it."

The Blacksmith grunted, his eyes tracing the symbols on the paper. Georgie leaned farther over the table, trying to get a glimpse of them.

"I'm not sure why he didn't come to you in the first place," Callum admitted. "I tried to send him to you, but he was...dodgy about it."

The Blacksmith glanced over his shoulder. "Here, boy." He held out the papers to him. "What do you make of these?"

Aware of Callum's surprised look, Georgie bit his lip. "I don't know..."

"Go on, son," said the Blacksmith encouragingly.

Eager to keep his father in good spirits, Georgie laid out the papers onto the table. In front of him lay a beautifully rendered sketch of the chain. Runes of all sorts danced around the diagram with little to no order, beyond some very insistent arrows pointing to every third, seventh, and ninth link.

"Did he say what it was for?" asked the Blacksmith.

"Not a word," replied Callum with a shrug. "Only that he needed it immediately."

"They're binding symbols," said Georgie, recognizing a few from the well-worn books his mother had owned. "Or at least, they start that way. I'm not sure what the rest of it means."

"Very good," said the Blacksmith.

Georgie traced his fingers along the lines, pausing at a circle in the corner. It was hastily drawn, but Georgie recognized it all the same. It was the same sort of symbol that had been drawn on the Old Woodsman's coffin.

"Was the man who ordered this at the funeral?" asked Georgie.

Callum and the Blacksmith shared a look. "He usually attends, yes," said Callum. "Can't imagine why, though. He keeps to himself."

"I'll take care of it," said the Blacksmith, clapping his large hand onto Callum's shoulder. "If you'd like to learn, I can show you."

Callum shook his head. "Thank you, sir, but no. I've got a dozen or so other tasks to get back to. I'd much rather you keep your secrets and your specialties."

"Very well. Shall I send it back to you once it's done?"

The handsome twenty-year-old shifted on his feet. "Well, like I said, all those other commissions… I'm a bit behind. I've already been away too long from my own forge as it is."

"I'll send my son," said the Blacksmith. "Georgie often does deliveries for me."

He did. It was a paltry skill of blacksmithing, but the only one that Georgie had perfected.

"A giant's blessing upon you, sir," said Callum, clasping the Blacksmith's hand. "I owe you."

The Blacksmith smiled. "The work is enough."

Chapter Three

Companions are rare in our line of work. There is a necessary aspect of rivalry amongst magic practitioners, and even greater amongst the Necromantic Arts. But should you find yourself a kindred spirit, they are invaluable. Even more so if they are still living.
  - The Dying Art of Necromancy, *Author Unknown*

* * *

The chain work was simple, as tried and true a method as any that centuries of Blacksmiths had perfected. Over the next three days, Georgie watched as his father shaped one iron link after the other, bending the iron rods around the anvil, hammering the edges into angled points, then, with the help of white-hot fire, molding the circle together.

The schematics that Callum had brought were very specific. The Blacksmith brooded over them, muttering under his breath and adding small hatch marks of his own. While most of the chain was made of solid round iron links, other parts needed to be stretched, long enough for the runes to be carved, but not so far that they would shatter.

With the iron cooled, the Blacksmith inscribed them. Georgie perched himself on top of the large stool, quickly handing his father one chisel after the other. With delicate precision, the runes took shape.

Runes to bind. Runes to hold. A ward against the cold so the iron wouldn't shatter on one, whilst the other held the ward against fire to twist.

"Seems he's thought of everything, hasn't he?" asked Georgie, still puzzling over the runes he didn't recognize.

The Blacksmith grunted in his chest. "They'll hold. These are simply for flavor." But even the Blacksmith's eyes widened as the runes lit up along the chain, sparking like blue lightning once the final line was set.

The exact same color and light from the funeral.

"It's done, then," he said, wiping his hands on his apron. "Well done, Georgie."

Georgie ducked his head bashfully beneath the praise as he gathered up the sketches.

"Your mother used to watch the same way," said the Blacksmith. "As if even the most common work were a marvel." Suddenly, the Blacksmith cleared his throat, blinking quickly.

Georgie felt the joy from the earlier praise slip away, as his father turned his back. For the last three days, Georgie had been keeping a close eye on him to make sure that his father wasn't slipping away into any more dark thoughts or getting lost in his work. Even if he couldn't work the forge, Georgie knew he was a tether, the lifeline that held his father towards the light.

"Go grab your things, son," the Blacksmith said gruffly. "I'll package this up."

* * *

The length of chain sat unceremoniously in a wheelbarrow. Aunt Elisa had offered to lend Georgie one of the goats and a cart, but the animals never behaved for Georgie. Part of him wanted to prove that while he wasn't strong enough for the forge, at the very least, he could push a wheelbarrow.

He pushed it all the way down the hill from the Blacksmith's forge and into the central square of the village. Here, the houses sat closer together, dotting the various hillsides with their white-plastered stone walls and cheery red roofing. The winding cobblestone streets were always bustling with trading, neighborly chats, and schoolchildren free for the summer shooed away from their homes by parents eager for a reprieve.

The excitement had a distinct air about it today as the villagers of Yoricsgrave were preparing for the annual festival simply known as the Strands. At the end of every summer, when the first cool breeze came down from the mountains, Yoricsgrave had a grand gathering. Yellow-gold streamers were being hung from the fenceposts, merchants were competing for the best spots for their booths, and a towering pole was being set up in the center of town. Georgie dodged through all of this, deep in thought, as the wheelbarrow rattled in his grasp over the bumpy streets.

His last conversation with his father loomed over Georgie like a storm cloud. He'd thought he'd done well in helping with the forge. But for what felt like the thousandth time, Georgie wondered what his mother would have done differently.

It was very difficult to try to be a person you only had vague memories of. Georgie could remember a few things. There was the lullaby that he often found himself humming beneath his breath, the memory of a warm embrace, and the sound of a woman's laughter. But where the memories should have been, only an ache remained.

He'd nearly made it to the edge of the square when a rough, overly familiar arm appeared over his shoulders.

"If it isn't Georgie Forgie!" Fitz, the village bully, yanked Georgie's head closer to his fist, jamming his knuckles into Georgie's scalp with painful accuracy. The wheelbarrow clattered to the ground with a thud. Two of Fitz's smirking minions watched, snickering, as Georgie tried to pull away.

Georgie was smaller, kept to himself, and didn't care about whatever hierarchy the village boys had conjured for themselves. Thus, he was their chosen target.

"Haven't seen you out and about in a while," said Fitz. "My boys and I were wondering when you'd scuttle out from your reading nook." Georgie tried to pull away again, but Fitz held on. "Must be learning something good, then. Are you going to share it with the class?"

Anger welled up inside of Georgie. "Let. Me. Go."

"What are you going to do? Run home to your mum? Oh, wait." Fitz rolled his eyes, belched in Georgie's face, and then shoved him to the ground. "She's gone off and died, hasn't she?"

Georgie felt a sharp sting in his knee, echoing the one in his heart that he tried so hard to not let the bullies see. They would never leave him alone if they knew how much it hurt. Satisfied that he'd been properly cowed, the bullies simply laughed at him and then ran off to bother someone else.

Georgie glared at the ground, his fists clenching and releasing with barely concealed rage. If his mother were alive, would they still have picked on him? He imagined a woman with bright-auburn hair, swooping in like a heroine from one of Aunt Elisa's stories. With a crack of magic on her fingertips, she would send the bullies running. Perhaps then she would pick Georgie off the ground herself and give him one of those warm embraces that he missed during the darkest of nights.

But it wasn't his mother's footsteps that approached. Instead, Ellory's slouching socks and scuffed boots stood beside him.

"Up you go, Georgie!" His little cousin pulled him up to his feet without a word about his sorry state.

"Thanks," Georgie muttered, brushing the dirt from his tunic.

"You could have taken him," Ellory said, trying to be helpful. "A few more years and you'll be enchanting circles around him." She peered down at the ripped patch on his knee. "Mum will *love* that."

"What are you doing out here?" Georgie asked.

Ellory shrugged. "I'm running an errand for Mum. What about you?"

"I'm delivering a commission for my da," Georgie explained. "Or trying to." He couldn't even walk across the village without getting picked on.

Ellory didn't mention it. "Where to?"

Georgie pointed in an eastward direction. "There's a man who lives up on the hilltops."

Ellory's head whipped around. "The cottage?"

"I think so," said Georgie. "He commissioned some spell work on some chains, and I—"

Ellory started bouncing up and down like an overexcited puppy. "I'm coming with you!"

* * *

Ellory marched in front of him, her large floppy hat now at her back while the wind tossed her chin-length brown hair. The breeze, stronger the closer they got to the hills, revealed the trouser legs from beneath Ellory's long green dress, reworked from one of Aunt Elisa's.

"It's probably for the local wizard," said Ellory. "They always need strange sorts of things like that."

"We have a wizard?" said Georgie.

Most villages along the road had one, or at least, the important villages did. There was a council of mages in the big city to the north. After the magicians studied there for a time, some were selected and sent to live in local villages.

But how could the quiet, sleepy town of Yoricsgrave have need of a wizard?

"When I ask around town about him, people are pretty miffed. Keeps to himself mostly." Ellory continued to rattle off her information. "He arrived about seven years ago. Apparently, he'd inherited the house on the hill."

Georgie thought it was strange that anyone should live so close to the base of the mountains. The Tombstone Mountains were tall and intimidating, jutting stones of gray, sharp and perilous. The shepherds whispered that you could hear the voices of the dead upon the wind.

It was safer to live in the valley, where the wind did not have as many bones to whistle between. The shepherds did well enough. Sheep did not rank very high in terms of intelligence, but after a few of them had gone missing, both they and the shepherds had learned which hills to avoid.

You're just going to deliver a commission, Georgie reminded himself in between deep breaths. *You're not staying for tea.*

Georgie paused in his steps. "Wait, you called him something else at the funeral."

Ellory grinned over her shoulder at him. "The Necromancer."

"Why do we have a Necromancer?"

"No idea!" Ellory said with absolute glee. "Weird, right? I can't wait to ask why."

Ellory was always asking questions. Often at the wrong times and to the wrong sort of people. There wasn't a single person to whom she wouldn't walk up to start a conversation with. No one was a stranger to Ellory, but if you were strange, you had a better chance of seeing her.

"How do you know he even *is* a Necromancer?"

His cousin's smile faded a bit, reluctant and shy. "I…I don't know if he's *actually* a Necromancer. That's just my theory. I was asking people. Apparently, this wizard only shows up at funerals, does the ritual that we saw, and that's it."

The various magicians each had their specialties. Enchanters would imbue objects with magical properties. Sorcerers were frontline fighters, fragile but effective as glass cannons. Wizards were scholars. Even some of the clergy had access to basic magics. But a magician that dealt with death?

Georgie suddenly felt very conflicted about delivering these chains to a Necromancer.

"Mum told me off for it," she said, suddenly sheepish and shy. "Told me not to go prying into other people's business or start nasty rumors. I told her I wouldn't, but it's just so mysterious and I—*stop!*" Ellory stood frozen in the middle of the road, her face suddenly pale.

Georgie dropped the wheelbarrow in alarm and ran to her. "What? What is it? What's wrong?" Frantically, he looked around for a dead body, a wild animal, or some other sort of horrid danger from the woods.

Ellory's hand slowly drifted down to her dress pocket. "I

forgot to deliver the rent money to Mrs. Havershem."

Georgie pressed a hand to his wildly pounding heart. "Giant's breath, is that all?"

Ellory's lower lip trembled. "I was supposed to deliver it before I found you. I completely forgot."

"It's all right, Ellory," Georgie said. "Surely you can deliver it tomorrow?"

Ellory shook her head fiercely. "She thinks I steal part of it. She has to count every coin whenever I deliver it, thinking that I'm grabbing treats on the way."

"Well, maybe I can go with you after we deliver the commission," said Georgie. "It won't take all that long, and then we can—"

"I have to go! Now!" Her notebook flew apart, scattering pages out onto the road as Ellory turned on her heel to run back down the mountainside.

"Ellory, wait!" Georgie cried out, but she was already gone.

Georgie hesitated. He didn't want Ellory to have to face her cranky landlady alone, but the village was safer than the woods after nightfall. The sun would set soon, and he was nearly there. Georgie sighed, gathering up what pages of Ellory's notebook he could, and returned to his wheelbarrow. He continued up the road, with only the creaking of the wheelbarrow wheels for company.

Chapter Four

Beware you who would dare knock upon a Necromancer's door. Their home is a tomb, their companions only bone, and death is always near. Visitors do not stay for long, nor are they welcome to.
- The Dying Art of Necromancy, *Author Unknown*

* * *

Georgie walked on for another fifteen minutes up the road until it turned to gravel. The small stones caused the wheelbarrow to jump and shake in his grasp, making such a racket that Georgie was certain it had echoed across the very mountains that surrounded them.

Cresting the hill, Georgie stopped to catch his breath and stretch out his aching hands. Behind him was a lovely view of the valley. Yoricsgrave sat quietly below. The fading light cast a favorable golden glow of home. He hoped Ellory had made it safely.

Turning away from the village, Georgie saw the house. Pressed up against the hillside and nestled amongst the trees, the cottage was hard to spot, the stonework hidden underneath the flourishing greenery that seemed to topple out from the roof itself. Dusty windowpanes peered out from between the vines, and the gentle glow of a dimly lit fire made the house flicker with a cozy light.

Off to the far right, farther into the mountains and separate from the main house, was a tall stone tower. It leaned perilously to one side, with the roof of the tower shaped in a haphazard peak. The entire building looked as though a child had built it from wooden blocks versus stone and mortar. There was a well in the courtyard, the chain to the bucket creaking slightly in the breeze, but otherwise, the house was silent.

Gathering his courage with the wheelbarrow, Georgie called out, "Hello?"

There was no answer.

"Everything will be fine," he muttered to himself, parking the wheelbarrow next to the well. "He might not even be a real Necromancer. Just Ellory's overactive imagination."

The entrance into the house was a simple wooden door with iron hinges. It would have been unremarkable if there weren't a golden skull with a ring hanging from its mouth nailed to the door.

Oh, how he wished he had gone with Ellory.

He reached up, quickly tapping the door with the ring. The skull didn't move, but Georgie couldn't help but wonder if the Necromancer was watching him through the skull's empty eye sockets. It seemed like the sort of thing a Necromancer would do.

The door opened as the final knock fell.

The inside of the house was lit softly by the dying embers of the fire and a few candles fluttering breathlessly in their sconces. It was a cluttered mess. Books and pieces of parchment lay scattered about, some with dust-covered spines. A large, comfortable armchair sat in the corner, covered in threadbare but serviceable blankets and cushions long dented with overuse. Bookshelves lined the walls, reaching towards the ceiling above. What little of the walls could be seen was decorated with frames of pinned moths with skull markings while a large taxidermy bear stood in the corner, one claw raised in the air as if in a friendly wave. Georgie steered clear of it and the disconcerting shine off of its still-sharp teeth. The entire house smelled of dust, something slightly acidic and the faint rot from an overwatered plant.

"Hello?" Georgie called again. He should leave. He should bring the chain work in, lay it inside the doorway, and leave.

But Georgie also knew how much his father was owed after such a commission. He couldn't return without payment. Besides, he'd never hear the end of it from Ellory if he ran away scared now.

As the silence lingered, Georgie's curiosity grew, drawing him towards the bookshelves. Each was stuffed with various volumes with colorful bindings mixed in with leather tomes. At least, Georgie *hoped* they were only leather. Some of the lighter ones looked suspicious.

He scanned the titles, not daring to touch the spines to brush the dust away. Most of them were obscure references.

Real World Magic.

Grave Mistakes and How to Avoid Them.

Undertaking the Task of Undertaking.

The Scriptorum Crematorium.

An Urnest Look at Alternative Burial Methods.

The Importance of Gravitas.

Georgie's attention wandered from the shelves towards a tall, cluttered desk in the corner. Scraps of parchment were strewn about while a chipped mug held a bird's worth of feather quills. But in the center of the desk, carefully kept separate from the mess, was yet another book left open, a leatherbound volume of midnight black.

Georgie stood on his tiptoes to look at the open pages. Alchemical symbols swirled across the page to a dizzying effect. The margins were covered in tiny, jotted notes in a handwriting that Georgie recognized from the chain work sketches.

"The forbidden art requires several things. Bones to shape, flesh to move, and blood to make a heart. It is the final two, mind and soul, that have yet to be acquired. We know this because it is impossible.

However, an impossibility to a mage is seen only as a time-consuming obstacle. It is theorized that if enough energy is poured into the subject that the mind may be formed. But it is a simple one, limited to the constraints of the emotions that created it."

Georgie swallowed, his throat suddenly dry. It couldn't be.

He slowly lifted the front cover from the desk, tilting his head to read the faded title.

The Dying Art of Necromancy.

Ellory had been right! The sheer joy of his cousin's validation was lost on him. He needed to leave. Now.

Georgie stepped back from the desk, wiping the chill from his hands on his pants when his foot landed on something small and brittle.

"*YEOW!*" There was a horrendous sharp screech from beneath. Georgie leapt around, tripping over a fast-moving shadow and against a bookshelf. With a mighty crash, the books toppled off the shelves. Georgie fell to the ground, covering his head as the books rained down on top of him.

There was another crash as the cottage door burst open.

"*Rigor mortis*! What happened?"

Stars danced across Georgie's vision, blurring the figure that loomed in the doorway.

The wizard, and it surely was he, looked younger than Georgie had expected. He was a gaunt fellow, perhaps in his mid-thirties, with fluffy, straw-colored hair that stuck out in odd directions over his sharp, prominent cheekbones and face.

He removed his black cloak, hanging it on a wobbling coatrack beside the door. Beneath it, he was dressed simply. The long, slim-cut trousers and a fitted shirt and jacket further accented his willowy frame. The man stumbled over to the shelf, looking about and muttering all the while. "Bone-cursed Void! What did I tell you about climbing the shelves?"

He set his hands on his hips and stared down at Georgie. "Who let *you* in?"

"The door was open, sir," Georgie said, removing a book from his head.

The wizard sighed. "I've got to fix that enchantment." He knelt down, gathering books in his arms, seemingly unperturbed at Georgie's sudden arrival. His eyes were a sharp ice blue, peering over a hooked nose. "I see you found the Void."

Georgie gulped. "The Void?"

A mournful meow answered him from the shadow in front of Georgie. The shadow turned, revealing two orbs of bright-green eyes. It was a cat, as ancient a cat as Georgie had ever seen. It matched its master with its equally slender body and jutting cheekbones. The cat was covered in patchy midnight-black fur, and one tooth perpetually hung out from the side of its mouth like a fang.

"Careful," the man warned. "There's never been a creature as spiteful as her."

He continued to gather the books off of Georgie and the floor, unconcerned with a proper order, and stacked them back onto the shelves. He reached out his hand, the same bone-white one Georgie had seen at the funeral. Georgie took it, surprised by how warm and human it felt.

With a quick turn on his heel, the wizard wandered over to unearth the stovetop. "Do you like tea? I don't get many visitors."

The man didn't seem to be aware of it, but a curious thing happened as he moved about the cottage. The pinned butterflies fluttered in their respective glass houses, as if even being near his proximity caused them a shudder of life. He opened up a wooden cabinet hanging from the wall. Several jars of herbs lay inside, some with freshly growing leaves spilling out from their containers . The plants opened up, standing straighter as he absentmindedly passed his hand over the m.

Georgie stood awkwardly by the shelves as the tea was prepared. He still wanted to run, but it would be bad manners to decline tea.

"Now, then," the wizard said, settling into the large armchair with a grateful sigh and a steaming mug. "Tell me, what do they call you?"

Georgie sat across from him, sinking into the plush sofa filled with cushions. A black speck of spite fell out from the shadows beneath it. With a hiss and a flick of her tail, the Void hopped onto the sofa, claiming her spot. Georgie dutifully slid towards the other end. "I'm Georgie." The wizard nodded at this, slowly sipping his tea. "What do they call you?"

The man glanced up from the rim of his cup. "The Necromancer."

Georgie sputtered into his drink, coughing to catch his breath. The Necromancer, an actual Necromancer, smiled in his chair, clearly waiting for him to either breathe or expire.

"When you're in my line of work, there's not a lot of room for subtlety. People are quick to point out that dead men tell no tales. But the live ones? They're the ones who do the talking." He took in Georgie's shock. "Clearly, it's happening less than I thought."

"You don't have a name?"

The Necromancer shrugged. "You sort of lose that once you gain your title at the Academy. 'Sir' is fine. 'Necromancer, sir' if you're feeling particularly respectful."

"Yes, of course…sir," said Georgie, his teacup now rattling nervously in his grasp.

The Necromancer continued to drink his tea. "What brings you here today, Georgie? Beyond the desire to rearrange my bookshelves?"

Georgie winced. "I'm delivering your commission, sir."

The man tilted his head, reminding Georgie of a curious vulture. "Commission?"

"You requested some chains made," said Georgie. "With particular spellwork?"

The Necromancer snapped his fingers. "Ah! Yes! I do remember. You have it, then?"

Georgie leapt to his feet, earning an angry yowl from the Void. "I do, sir! Let me get it!" Before the man could protest, Georgie set his tea down on the table and ran outside.

When he was far from the door, he took a moment to catch his breath.

A Necromancer, as honest a truth as stone. But why? What

was he doing here?

More importantly, what was Georgie doing out here when *a Necromancer* was waiting for him to return?

"You can do this, you can do this, you can do this," he muttered beneath his breath with each step towards the wheelbarrow. The chains were heavy and bound tightly in a woolen sack. Georgie hefted it over his shoulder like a bag of metal grain. Was it the weight or fear that made his legs wobble so?

The man sat inside, still sipping his tea, when Georgie stumbled over the threshold once more. Even with all the noise from hauling the chains inside, it was only once Georgie had dropped it in front of him that the wizard took notice.

Georgie collapsed on the sofa, out of breath. "Here, sir."

The Necromancer set down his teacup to open the sack in front of him. Inspecting the commission with a sharp look, he scoured over every inch of the chain , murmuring to himself.

"Water and rust, heat and flame. Good. Very good. Grooves are deep enough. They'll hold." Still looking at the chains, he held out his hand to Georgie. "The man I left this with told me he would deliver it." His eyes narrowed. "You don't look much like him at all."

Georgie rubbed at the back of his neck. "No, sir. Callum asked my da, Alistair Smith, to help him."

"Who knew such a small town could hold so many smiths?" the Necromancer murmured. "Is your father a man to be trusted?"

Georgie's heart stuttered a bit. Did the Necromancer know about his father's moods? Was it bad enough already that others were taking notice again? "Yes, sir. Of course he is, sir."

The Necromancer nodded, satisfied. "My sketches, please."

Georgie reached into his shirt pocket and pulled them out.

"My da made a few modifications. He said that if you need any more, he'll have to—"

The Necromancer threw the parchment over his shoulder and into the fire.

"What are you doing?" Georgie exclaimed as the parchment caught immediately and the intricate sketches curled away into ash.

"Decluttering," was all the Necromancer said before carefully winding the chain back into the sack and wiping his hands off on his shirt.

The door shuddered with three loud knocks.

"No bodies here!" the Necromancer called out before chuckling to himself.

"Georgie? Georgie, are you in there?"

Georgie leapt up from his seat. "It's my cousin, Ellory."

The Void hissed as the knocking continued rapidly on the door.

"She's very persistent," said the Necromancer.

"You have no idea."

The Necromancer nodded for Georgie to let her in. Ellory fell inside, her ear still pressed to the door. Georgie grabbed her arm to help her up. "Are you all right?"

Ellory's eyes darted around, taking in her surroundings as quickly as she could. "I'm fine."

The Necromancer gave a cheerful wave from where he sat, but he didn't speak further.

"It's getting late," said Georgie, pointedly ignoring Ellory's squeak of curious protest. "We should get back."

"I agree," said the Necromancer. "You'll want payment, I imagine."

Ellory gave Georgie a look as the Necromancer went into the

other room. Georgie didn't know where to begin, so he simply gave a shrug.

"Here you are," said the Necromancer, reappearing with a small black satin pouch that jingled with coin. He dropped it into Georgie's hand. "Until next time." Then he took both Georgie and Ellory by the shoulders, spun them around, and quickly thrust them out the door.

Chapter Five

There are a variety of schools of magic. Abjuration for the protective, Conjuration for the imaginative, Divination for the religious, Enchantment for the controlling charismatic, Evocation for those who prefer their studies to be elemental, Illusion for the tricksters and finally, Necromancy. Necromancy is for the determined and the desperate.

  - The Dying Art of Necromancy, *Author Unknown*

* * *

Georgie could feel Ellory's eyes burrowing holes into his face. She stayed silent, waiting until they were farther down the hill and a safe distance away from the Necromancer's cottage. "So?"

"You were right." Georgie dug in his bag, handing her the loose papers from her notebook that he had collected earlier. "He's a Necromancer."

Ellory's face lit up in delight. "I knew it! Tell me everything that happened." She grabbed her notebook , stuffing the papers inside, and immediately started jotting down notes. Georgie explained the day's events, the books he'd seen, the interaction with the Void, and a little of his conversation with the Necromancer afterwards.

"Were you in there for a while?" asked Ellory, as excited as a bloodhound with a fresh scent. "What did the tea taste like? Do you think he's human or a reanimated skeleton?"

Georgie didn't know the answers to all of her questions but enjoyed entertaining his cousin nonetheless.

Aunt Elisa and Ellory joined them for dinner that night. The night breeze whistled gently in through the open windows, mixing with the warm smell of fresh bread. Aunt Elisa moved about the kitchen easily, stirring the stew on the stove, chopping up more vegetables, and instructing Ellory. As comfortable as a captain on her ship, Aunt Elisa was good at what she did. Georgie knew just how much that meant to his father.

Aunt Elisa wasn't married. The way Ellory had told it, her parents had been madly in love, but her father had gone to seek his fortune before proposing. Ellory had already been on the way when word had come that he had disappeared. Aunt Elisa had been close with Adelaide, who'd insisted that she stay nearby despite the rumors, whispers, and pitying looks.

Aunt Elisa was a proud woman, but even she couldn't raise a child without any funds. Though Aunt Elisa had insisted it wasn't necessary, Georgie knew the Blacksmith set aside money for her and Ellory each month. The arrangement seemed to suit both parties just fine.

"I won't be able to stop by for the next few days," said Aunt Elisa after they'd begun eating. "Mrs. Havershem has ordered an entire dowry's worth of bed linens and needs them prepared before her daughter's wedding."

"I thought you stopped taking other work," said the Black-smith curiously.

Aunt Elisa looked down at her plate, her voice suddenly small. "She's raising rent. Again."

The Blacksmith's hand gripped his knife with unusual fierceness. "Why?"

"I'm sorry," said Ellory, sinking lower in her seat. "It's my fault. I thought I'd remembered in time, but she—"

Aunt Elisa kissed her daughter on the head. "It's not your fault, love, not at all."

"Did she give a reason?" the Blacksmith asked.

"She simply wants the money for those bed linens."

"And then forces you to embroider them for less."

Aunt Elisa shrugged. "I can pay it. I can send Ellory to do a couple of the chores so the house isn't a total mess by the time I return. You won't even know I'm gone."

The Blacksmith grumbled under his breath, a dark cloud covering his face.

"How did your errand go today, Georgie?" asked Aunt Elisa, tactfully changing the conversation.

Georgie pushed the potatoes around on his plate. "All right. I met the Necro—"

Ellory kicked him from underneath the table.

"The wizard," corrected Georgie. "He's nice."

"I'd have thought he would have moved on years ago," said Aunt Elisa, tapping her cheek. "Yoricsgrave is a bit of a dead end for a magic practitioner."

Ellory snorted, so Georgie poked her in the side. Neither of them were doing a very good job of keeping the secret.

"Your mum, Adelaide, had a bit of magic to her," said Aunt Elisa, serving the last of the rolls out to everyone. "She used to visit the old wizard on the hill before he passed. What was his name?"

"Sardis," the Blacksmith replied, his voice as low as thunder.

"That's the one!" said Aunt Elisa, ever a ray of sunshine. "He wasn't a kind man, but from what she told me, he was all alone for many years up there. She would visit him even when he'd chased the rest of the village away." She smiled to herself. "Stubborn to the end, my sister. Eventually, he gave in and taught her a few tricks. Then, when he finally passed, she looked after the cottage grounds for a while until the new wizard arrived."

"Why would she want to learn magic from a miserable old goat?" Ellory asked.

Aunt Elisa gave her daughter a wry look. "Mind your manners with the dead." The proverb was as old as the mountains, so Ellory paid it little mind. "Adelaide wanted to go to the College of Magi," Aunt Elisa continued. "She would read any books she could get her hands on in order to learn a new trick or two."

Georgie took a new look at the cluttered bookshelves that surrounded them. He'd read them a dozen times over, looking for memories of his mother before they faded away. "What happened?"

The Blacksmith cleared his throat, his eyes suddenly downcast and blinking rapidly. Aunt Elisa reached for his hand, placing hers on top. "She fell in love."

There was a long pause of silence until the Blacksmith pulled his hand away. He wiped his face before he stood. "Thank you, Elisa. Please excuse me." His father's weighted sadness left the room, taking a bit of the warmth with him.

Aunt Elisa watched him go, her eyes lingering on the doorway. "I thought he was getting better at talking about her."

"He's fine," said Georgie, even if it felt like a lie.

Aunt Elisa turned back in her seat to the table, offering a

smile. "I'm sure he is."

But the Blacksmith still hadn't returned by the time Aunt Elisa and Ellory were returning home.

His aunt noticed Georgie's concern. "It'll be all right, Georgie."

Georgie nodded, trying to keep a brave face.

Aunt Elisa knelt down, cupping his face in her hands. "You take so much after her, Georgie. More than you know."

With Aunt Elisa and Ellory gone, Georgie was left alone in the quiet house, with only the distant sounds of a hammer falling from the forge beyond.

He paced back and forth. Things were getting worse. Aunt Elisa was usually the balm to the Blacksmith's wounds, so quick and able to tend to his moods. But not this time. Georgie loved his aunt. She was kind and loving and, after years of tending to the Blacksmith by himself, a true miracle. If he wasn't enough, and his Aunt Elisa, as close to a saint as Georgie knew, wasn't, then what was? And if the Necromancer hadn't come to his da, the finest Blacksmith in Yoricsgrave, for a commission, did that mean he'd noticed his father's depression as well?

Georgie had never really been at sea, but in all the books he'd read, nothing came quite as close to describing grief as a storm. You learned your knots, stocked up on supplies, and you sailed as close to the wind and sun as you could get. But the storms always came anyway, and it was all you could do to batten down the hatches. Hold on tight and wait for it to pass. The Blacksmith's grief was a difficult thing. It overwhelmed him, dragging him beneath dark waves.

It meant that his father was gone for a night. Sometimes two, only to arrive clearly worse for wear when he did come home. It meant that food was sometimes scarce because his father could barely get out of bed and refused to see any sort of doctor. It meant that dirty dishes stacked up until gnats buzzed about them. Or that laundry would pile up until Georgie figured out how to wash it himself. He knew his father had left only so that Georgie wouldn't have to see his grief or hear his weeping in the long stretches of night without any sleep.

Georgie had learned to look after himself and, in time, had looked after his father as well. He'd tried to reach his father with whatever he could. A small meal, a quiet presence, or even trying to talk about things. Each and every attempt would simply be shut down as he slipped further and further into depression.

Georgie couldn't let that happen again.

There had to be something he could do. Something that he wasn't thinking of. If he was supposed to hold magic, like his mother, what would she have done? If only she were here so that he could talk to her. He had so many questions to ask . What would she have done differently if she were here with them? The same chill from the tower crept over Georgie again as the answer appeared in front of him.

What if she were alive?

If he could bring her back, that would solve his father's grief. He wouldn't have to be sad anymore. Aunt Elisa wouldn't have to work so hard, and Georgie...

Georgie could finally have a mother.

Chapter Six

Grief is the great enemy of Necromancy. It is our most constant foe and the source of all the world's trouble. But it is also our lifeline. Why else would Necromancy exist if grief did not?
  - The Dying Art of Necromancy, *Author Unknown*

* * *

Georgie went to see the Necromancer the next morning.

It was depressingly simple to slip out of the house without his father noticing. The Blacksmith was already at the forge, and Georgie struggled to remember if he'd even come back inside last night at all.

Georgie had practiced all last night on what he would say to the Necromancer. Should he bring his report cards from school to prove that he was an excellent student? Would he have to beg?

All that Georgie knew was that he couldn't afford to be told 'no.'

But with each step up the gravel path towards the Necromancer's cottage, Georgie's doubt grew.

What could he offer to someone who held the power to resurrect the dead?

The cottage was the same as he'd left it, the odd, melancholy feeling hovering about it like dust motes in the morning light. Gathering his courage and the cold metal ring in the skull's mouth, Georgie knocked on the door.

This time, the door did not open on its own. The skull leered down at him, prodding at his courage as if to say, *Well, now what?*

Georgie thought back to the stories Aunt Elisa would tell. A brave hero would do whatever it took, even if it meant barging through the door. But that seemed, to Georgie, quite rude, so he would simply have to be brave enough to wait.

Several moments passed before he started hearing shuffling from behind the door. There was an insistent murmuring behind it, as well as a few loud, indignant yowls from a cat before the door creaked open.

The Necromancer stood in the doorway, his hair splayed out to one side as if he'd slept on it wrong. The Void wrapped herself around his ankles with terrifying fondness.

"Ah, Gerald," said the man.

Georgie blinked. "No. It's—"

"Geoffrey!" said the Necromancer with a snap of his fingers.

"No," he replied, careful to keep his tone civil. "It's Georgie."

The Necromancer's eyes narrowed before opening wide. "Oh. Right. Georgie. The errand boy." He leaned against the doorway, crossing his arms. "What can I do for you?"

This was it. The moment Georgie had been waiting for. In the end, all of his careful words flew away, leaving the honest truth. "I want to learn Necromancy."

The tall man stared down at Georgie for a long moment with

his pale-blue eyes. "Come again?"

"I want to learn Necromancy," Georgie repeated. "I need your help."

"Tell me, what interest does someone as young as you have in Necromancy? Did someone die before you could take your revenge?"

"No, sir."

"Are you haunted by a ghost and need to release its hold upon your home so that you can get a moment's peace?"

"No, sir." Georgie paused. "Does that happen a lot?"

"More often than you think," the Necromancer replied distantly. "Especially in this town." He leaned in very closely. "You're not some cruel little boy who likes to pluck the legs off a spider, are you?"

"What? No!"

"I thought not," he replied. "You'd be more keen than frightened if that were the case."

"I'm n-not frightened."

The Necromancer raised a single nearly translucent eyebrow before his gaze purposefully fell on Georgie's trembling legs.

Georgie snapped his heels together and gritted his teeth. "I'm not."

"You have your whole life ahead of you still. If you're lucky, it'll be many years before you ever have need of a Necromancer," he said with a yawn as he closed the door.

Georgie was being dismissed. The Necromancer wasn't even interested in hearing why.

"I need to bring someone back to life," said Georgie, sticking his foot in the doorway.

The door thumped to a halt as the Necromancer stared at him. "What did you say?"

"I need to bring someone back to life," Georgie repeated.

The Necromancer grabbed Georgie's shoulder, his eyes darting back and forth across the yard as if he expected someone else to be listening. "I think you ought to come inside for this conversation."

The Necromancer made a squawking sound as he tripped over the Void. "*Mortem oppetere*, Void! Get out of the way!"

The black cat hissed back before giving a decidedly irritated flick of her tail as she ran deeper into the house.

The Necromancer didn't completely shut the door, leaving the sunlight outside to peer through the crack with its own curiosity. "The Void will scream at me otherwise," he explained, gesturing for Georgie to take a seat.

"A Necromancer's duty is to guard and protect the dead," he said, sitting across from Georgie. "Not to utilize them for our whims." There was a practiced air about this statement, as if he'd spoken it aloud many, many times.

"It's not a whim," said Georgie. "It's incredibly important."

"And what makes you so certain you're up to the task?"

"You said I was good at developing new symbols. You saw what I did on the chain work? Doesn't that mean anything?"

"It means you're a blossoming engineer and inventor," he replied with a wave of his hand. "It does not mean that you will be able to do what thousands of years' worth of Necromancy has deemed impossible."

"But the book," Georgie insisted, pointing back towards the still-open tome. "On your desk! You're studying it too."

The Necromancer's eyes narrowed. "I was reading as a refresher."

"Please, you have to help me!" Georgie's desperation rose in his chest. It cracked his voice in his throat. "My da. He needs her!"

The Necromancer paused. "Your mother, is it? How did she die?"

"It was an accident," Georgie said hollowly. "She went out for a walk when she got caught in a storm. It must have turned her around, or she slipped." He hung his head. "They found her dead at the bottom of one of the cliffs two days later."

"When did this happen?"

Georgie wiped his nose with his sleeve. "Six years ago."

The Necromancer was still for a long time before giving a bone-weary sigh. He reached into his pocket and produced a handkerchief, passing it to Georgie. "I'm sorry for your loss, boy. But I cannot help you. Not with this."

He'd failed, then. He'd done the brave and bold thing, and he still hadn't come any closer. All the magic that he carried, the only remnant left of his mother, hadn't been enough. Worse still, Georgie knew he needed to get back. Even if it was only to be there to watch his father disappear once more underneath his grief. The only chance he'd had to help was gone, shut in his face as silent and cold as his own mother's tombstone.

Georgie wiped his tears away before handing back the handkerchief. "Sorry. I didn't mean to take so much of your time, sir."

"One can't really put a time limit on distress." The Necromancer's voice was soft. "Or grief, for that matter."

Georgie stood, giving a small bow to try to hide his brimming tears underneath his hair. As he went to leave, he heard the fire *whoosh* up again from fresh kindling. The used handkerchief caught quickly. The firelight lit the Necromancer's face in strange, flickering lights of ruby red, far deeper than any natural fire could produce.

"Georgie! Wait!" The Necromancer hadn't moved from his seat, his brow furrowed in deep contemplation. "I cannot bring your mother back," he said slowly, testing each word with his tongue and teeth. "But I can teach you."

Georgie stumbled back towards him. "You'll do it? You'll actually teach me?"

The Necromancer sat thoughtfully, scratching his chin. "It *is* curious timing. That woman has been after me to take an apprentice for years now. Personally, I thought there was no one in this isolated town worth the trouble. But two minds are better than one. You might be of use to me after all. However, it will take a significant portion of my time to teach you, so it may be necessary for you to assist me with other matters." He paused for a moment, his keen eyes narrowing at Georgie. "What would you give me in return?"

Georgie's mind immediately leapt to the worst conclusion, his stomach churning with panic. "Would it cost me my life?"

"Oh, I don't need your life," said the Necromancer. "Only your corpse once you've expired!" There was a long, awkward pause before the Necromancer burst into a laugh. "Just kidding! We certainly don't do that anymore." He quickly returned to his morning tea, averting his gaze and giving a loud sip. "Errands, mostly. You do that sort of thing, right? My own work keeps me here, but I could always use someone to fetch a few things."

Right. Errands. Georgie could do that. "Certainly, sir. Whatever you need."

The Necromancer gave a wide grin, echoing the skull on his door. "Well, then, congratulations, Georgie. You're now the apprentice of the Necromancer."

Chapter Seven

Secrecy is the necessary spine of Necromancy from which all the rest of the Necromantic Arts are connected. A Necromancer cannot divulge his experiments with the general public, as historically, this has caused incidents of public outrage, overdrawn and costly legal proceedings, banishment and being burnt at the stake.
- The Dying Art of Necromancy, *Author Unknown*

* * *

Georgie had a lot to think about during his long walk back to the village.

It had been naïve of him to assume that the Necromancer would readily do the impossible and resurrect his mother if he asked. He'd been bold enough to approach the man as if he'd been a fairy godmother, but the Necromancer hardly fit that description.

Perhaps he could convince him in time. Or perhaps, as the Necromancer had said, two minds were better than one. If he was patient, proved that he was a good student, perhaps they could discover the way to subvert the impossibility of resurrection.

And if they didn't? Well, there was always the Necromancer's library.

Georgie had often found that, where his own teachers lacked, the library was a vast source of information. While his peers in school were struggling through an old world play, Georgie finished such things in an hour, reaching for a larger compendium. Fitz often laughed at him for the large books that he carried around. Meanwhile, the Blacksmith had to remind Georgie that he wasn't allowed to carry six or more books in his bag at any given time or he would ruin his back. The words from the open book on the Necromancer's desk came back to Georgie.

"An impossibility to a mage is seen as a time-consuming obstacle."

But if the Necromancer wasn't willing to teach him, perhaps his library would.

* * *

Ellory was waiting for him when he got home, looming in the doorway.

"Where were you this morning?" The shorter girl managed to look very intimidating despite the bandana over her hair, the stained apron, and the dripping mop still clutched in her hand.

Georgie hesitated. "I took a walk," he said. "It's nice out."

Ellory put her free hand on her hip. "You took a walk because it's nice out?"

"Yeah," said Georgie, pushing past her to go inside. "That's all."

"You're a terrible liar, Georgie Smith."

He flinched. "Ellory, please." But the look in Ellory's eyes was one that Georgie was all too familiar with. If she didn't get a sufficient answer, she'd go snooping herself.

"Fine," he said. "I went to the Necromancer's."

Ellory was unfazed. She'd probably guessed as much. "And?"

Georgie chewed on the inside of his cheek. "He offered to tutor me."

Ellory actually squealed with glee. She promptly dropped the mop and pulled her notebook out from the apron, battering him excitedly with it. "Georgie! This is incredible!"

But even as his cousin celebrated, Georgie felt unsure.

What would Ellory and Aunt Elisa do once his mother was back from the dead? Surely, all that he'd heard about Adelaide would mean that she would still be kind to them, but his father wouldn't need the help anymore. Ellory was ever so fond of her mother. They had a closeness that Georgie envied. Despite Ellory's enthusiasm, he doubted she would want her mother replaced.

"Hey, Georgie? You still in there?" Ellory waved her hand in front of him. "Your face got all sad there for a moment."

He swallowed, trying to ignore the bitterness of the lie on his tongue. "It's nothing."

"Is this about Fitz still? Because he's an idiot, and you don't need to worry about him. I'd bet he'd never have even made it over the garden wall. Never mind hold his own in conversation with a Necromancer."

That made Georgie smile. "True enough."

Ellory opened her notebook, her pencil poised and ready. "Why are you interested in Necromancy?"

Georgie felt his stomach flip. "I want to learn magic," he blurted out. "Any magic. It's what my mum was good at, wasn't it? If I can learn about it…maybe…maybe it would help me feel closer to her."

Ellory stared deep into his eyes. He didn't know what she found there that satisfied her, but she drew back all the same. "Guess it's not your fault that all we've got is a Necromancer." She tapped her chin with her pencil. "Will you share your notes with me?"

She'd already called him out on one secret he hadn't intended to tell her. Would he really be able to keep the rest? The Necromancer had sternly warned him a dozen times over that he was not to tell a single soul, dead or alive, the specifics of what he learned. But Ellory was the smartest and cleverest person Georgie knew. The Necromancer hadn't met her for long, but if anyone could keep a secret, maybe even help crack the formula for raising the dead, surely she could.

"Of course," Georgie promised.

Ellory beamed at him, wrapping her arms around him for a fierce hug. "You're my favorite cousin!"

"I'm your only cousin," he reminded her.

"That too!" She gave him an extra squeeze.

"There's still one problem, though," said Georgie. "What do I tell Da?"

Ellory pulled back, her face serious. "You can't tell him. Or my mum."

"What do you mean? Of course I have to tell them."

"I mean, you can't tell them he's a Necromancer!"

"You don't think they know?"

Ellory threw up her hands. "If they knew, do you think they'd let you keep going back?"

"But *you* knew!"

"I'm very clever," she said slowly. "I ask questions that the adults are too afraid to ask." Ellory gave a shrug. "Maybe just call him 'the wizard.' Everyone else does. Your da doesn't need to know the specifics. Besides, it's not like he'll have you raising the dead on your first day."

Georgie certainly hoped not.

***

The sun began to set, and Ellory had left hours ago to go back home. But the Blacksmith was still at the forge.

Georgie tried to be patient but found himself pacing in the too big and too quiet house, with only the ever-present *tick, tick, tick* of the clock on the wall to remind him of the passage of time. He'd made himself dinner, grabbing what leftovers he could out of the icebox.

It's fine, he told himself. *Da is fine.*

But the hours passed slowly, and his father still hadn't come inside.

Georgie gathered up his cloak and a lantern. The orange glow of the forge shone brightly in the evening light, late-summer fireflies blinking lazily in time with his father's hammer.

The Blacksmith didn't notice him come in. His back was to the door as he stood bent over some smoldering bright-orange piece of metal. The plate of lunch still sat untouched on the table.

"Da?"

The Blacksmith gave a few last heavy whacks with his hammer before he turned. Wiping the sweat off his brow, he looked pleased to see Georgie. "Hello, boy."

"It's getting late," said Georgie, nodding over his shoulder to the encroaching darkness.

The Blacksmith blinked for a moment, realizing how much

he'd lost of the day. "So it is." He took his work, setting it to cool.

Georgie nodded to the bucket of fresh water in the corner. The Blacksmith took the cloth inside and wiped his face and arms with it, then washed his hands.

"You've been working a lot today," Georgie said carefully.

The Blacksmith gave a soft laugh. "Time ran away from me, it seems. I've taken a few extra jobs to save up for something."

The Blacksmith took a long drink from the waterskin, the water dribbling down his beard. "I trust you kept yourself busy today."

Georgie didn't know how his news would go over. Not because his father would disapprove, but if he really was doing poorly, who would be there to take care of him?

"In a way," he said, tracing the leftover water rings into half-sketched runes on the table. "I went up to see the Ne—the wizard. He offered to tutor me."

"Tutoring? Don't you want to spend the last of your summer months doing something else besides studying?" asked the Blacksmith. "There's still time before school starts. Perhaps you could go out and run around with the other boys your age."

Georgie's newly scraped knee stung beneath his father's suggestion. "I think I'd rather learn more about magic, if that's all right with you."

"Does he expect payment for this?"

Georgie shook his head. "Just a couple of errands. I don't think he makes it into town much."

The Blacksmith sat down with a long sigh, rubbing at his brow. "I suppose it couldn't hurt." His face crinkled into a tired smile. "It'll be strange not having you around, though."

"I won't be gone long each day," Georgie said quickly. "And

I'm not far. If you need anything, I can always run back to help."

"Georgie." The Blacksmith put his heavy hand on his son's shoulder. "I'll be all right. It might be good for you to get out of the house. And to be studying magic? Well, your mother… She'd be proud of you."

If this worked, Georgie hoped to be able to hear that from her.

Chapter Eight

It has been said that those who do not learn from history are doomed to repeat it. It is a weighty phrase often wielded by philosophers, historians, and politicians. A Necromancer understands that tragic history is a series of miserable failings from their predecessors and studies history to improve upon sloppy work.
 - The Dying Art of Necromancy, *Author Unknown*

* * *

The Blacksmith told Georgie that the best thing to do was often the first step in front of you. Well, the first few steps were to make it on time.

In a way, it felt like his first day of school. Normally, he loved the thrill of a new notebook, took excellent care of his quill and additional sets of ink, and enjoyed the crisp, cool air of the fall that promised new things.

It was quite a different feeling approaching a house, knowing that you wanted to bring your mother back from the dead. He didn't know what that entailed.

Would the Necromancer force Georgie to go into the grave-yard, alone, and at night, for some sinister purpose? To dig up graves or collect bones? The sweat on his back from the late-summer sun turned cold, with each terror more terrible than the last. Was it his imagination or did the lazy curling smoke from the chimney look like a ghost? Or was it a literal one?

Georgie shook his head fiercely. This would not do. He couldn't be a scared rabbit if he wanted the Necromancer's help. Aunt Elisa had said that his mother had been brave. It was why she had gone out walking late at night. It was why few had worried when she hadn't come back right away during the storm.

If Georgie's mother had been brave, well, he figured he could be brave about bringing her back if he needed to. Besides, hadn't she walked this very path before to help the previous Necromancer? The thought of literally following in his mother's footsteps gave him courage. If Georgie was successful in his quest, he would be able to return home by his mother's side.

The door was open when Georgie arrived. The Void lay at the doorstep, stretched across the threshold like a final ill omen.

"Hello, Void," Georgie said politely. "Can I come in?"

The cat looked up at him through her hooded green eyes. With no rush, or any semblance of respect for punctuality, the Void stretched out farther.

Georgie tried to step over her, only for the cat to jump up beneath his foot with a loud hiss.

With a sharp cry, Georgie fell backward, landing painfully on his rear end as the Void skittered back into the house.

The Necromancer popped his head out of the doorway. "Aha! You're here!"

Georgie stood, giving up his dignity to dust off the back of his pants. "Yes, sir."

"Come, come in! We have much to learn today!" The Necromancer had a different sort of energy about him . His eyes were alight and eager as he graciously took Georgie's pack and brought him over to the table.

There was a large stack of books on one end while on the other side sat three different types of ink and what looked like an entire bird's worth of feather quills.

"Always best to be prepared," said the Necromancer sheepishly.

Georgie took his seat on the provided stool and grabbed a piece of blank parchment and a feather quill. Ellory had made him promise, three times, that he would take notes.

"Before we begin, there are a few rules that will need to be obeyed if you are to continue on as my apprentice," said the Necromancer. "Rules that are to be followed without question and without delay."

"Yes, sir," said Georgie.

The Necromancer listed them off on his slender fingers. "One, our lessons will always be in the morning, and I will send you home long before dusk. Two, you are never to wander the foothills near this cottage at night. Three, I will have business to attend to periodically throughout the day. I expect you to stay focused on your studies, even if I am away for the moment. Finally, number four, you are not to practice anything which you learn in this house without strict supervision. Is that clear?"

Georgie nodded. He certainly would never dream of walking the foothills at night. The third request stuck out to him. He might have a chance to get a closer look at the Necromancer's library after all. But the last request was the trickiest of all. Still, he could promise not to break it, at least not today. "Yes, sir. I understand."

"Excellent." The Necromancer clapped his hands together. "Today's lesson is on history!"

Georgie dutifully wrote 'The History of Necromancy' at the top of his parchment. The ink was a deep black, the finest Georgie had ever written with.

"Necromancy is a delicate art that has been refined through the ages," said the Necromancer. "Its popularity has fluctuated, but it remains an important magical art." The Necromancer went to a wooden door at the end of the wall. "Now, I could have you read a dozen different tomes, lecture you for hours, but the greatest benefit of Necromancy is that you have the opportunity to learn from direct sources." With a grand flourish, he opened it. There was a brief shudder before a pile of bones collapsed out of the closet and on top of the Necromancer.

Georgie leapt up from his seat, the ink wobbling precariously on the table. "You said you didn't keep bodies here!"

The Necromancer wrestled with the pile of bones, eventually setting them upright onto a metal pole with wheels. "This is a skeleton." The Necromancer noted Georgie's alarm. "What? You didn't expect to speak with the dead on your first day?"

Georgie gulped.

"Don't worry, boy," said the Necromancer. "Herbert here is a bit of an old hat, the finest historian of the Necromantic Arts. His information is a bit dated, as is the nature of things, but he is invaluable when it comes to historical matters."

The Necromancer wheeled over the skeleton, plucking it off the rack as if it were a waltz partner. He did a couple of turns about the room before settling it down in the armchair.

"Do you…Do you do this often?" Georgie asked.

The Necromancer grinned. "Do you think I'd keep him in the closet if I did? No. Herbert here is on loan from the College of

Magi. Besides"—the Necromancer patted the skeleton's skull—"Ol' Herbert here was a volunteer. One of the first, actually."

"Volunteer?"

"To become a Necromantic Archive." The Necromancer twisted the skull fully around, pointing to a series of engraved markings on the back of it. Georgie slowly approached, doing his best to ignore the glaring-white bones to take a closer look.

"It's not information that the College widely spreads, but there are whole hosts of skulls lining the shelves of the libraries for such a purpose as this," the Necromancer explained. "Herbert here likes to talk with his hands, so we keep him intact."

He shooed Georgie aside so that he could kneel in front of the skeleton. "Are you ready?" he asked.

Georgie nodded, his mouth too dry to speak.

The Necromancer closed his eyes for a moment, placing his hands on either side of the skull. *"Lausu totuus menneiltä ajoilta. Kerro mitä olet nähnyt ja kuullut."*

Several things happened at once. The candles flickered lower in their sconces as he chanted under his breath. The winds picked up, fluttering the pages of the books in the room as the pinned butterfly wings beat rapidly in their frames in the same rhythm as a heartbeat. The Necromancer continued to chant, even as the Void yowled in protest, darting off to hide. Georgie wished he could do the same. A *whoosh* of breath escaped the Necromancer's lips.

There was a moment of silence. Then the skeleton began to move.

It started with a twitch in the fingerbones, then a loud crack as Herbert straightened his neck. The empty eye sockets passed over Georgie.

"Hello, Herbert," said the Necromancer, not at all disturbed by the undead horror sitting casually before him. "It's been a bit."

The skeleton's jaw dropped open as if he were taking a breath, but with no lungs with which to do so, he shut it once more.

The Necromancer nodded in Georgie's direction. "This is my new apprentice."

The skeleton shifted suddenly, the empty eye sockets finding Georgie in the gloom. A gust of wind hid a breathy voice, quiet and distant.

There once was a clever man who thought himself a spider to the Fates.
For every single thread they snipped, he'd snatch and hold in place.

Death-Weaver, the King named him, a god amongst wizards.
But the Fates are ever patient and sharpened their scissors.

The world was at war, giants crushing town and home.
The King called upon the Death-Weaver to answer the threat —
alone.

Death-Weaver pulled the threads of fate, knotting giant's life to bone.
He led the undead giant to the enemy camp, as if he were returning home.

The giants did not question it, so great was the loss and grief.
That any sight of a friendly face, undead or otherwise, gave them much relief.

But their joy was short-lived, as they soon would learn
When Death-Weaver bid the undead draw his knife and stab them

in return.

For every giant that fell, Death-Weaver raised them up once more.
Chaos ensued. Severed limbs flew and endless rivers of blood poured.

The giants slew themselves, falling where they'd once slept.
But Death-Weaver's victory was sundered as the Fates saw their chance and leapt.

The man held too many life threads, his own hands now tied.
Tangled and bound, the clever man's own thread snapped — he died.

Stillness fell over the valley, as walls of bone became stone.
The man lies there still to this day, never to atone.

Be careful, you who seek the power to bind fate's severed threads to bone.
The lesson here, dear Necromancer, is that death always comes for its own.

Herbert shuddered with the final words drifting in the air before collapsing back into the chair, his skeletal mouth left gaping open.

The Necromancer sat back on his heels. "And there you have it! Herbert's party trick."

Herbert's warning was as sharp as ice on Georgie's skin. His teeth chattered, as if he'd spent hours outside in the winter without a coat. The cold muddled his thoughts, making it hard for him to grasp what he'd seen. "That's…That's it?"

The Necromancer slowly turned to Georgie, one brow raised in disbelief. "That wasn't enough for you?"

"No. I mean, yes. It was really…something. I just—"

Georgie continued to stammer, rubbing at his arms to warm up. The Necromancer picked up the skeleton once more and headed towards the closet.

"Those are the first words every Necromancer hears when they begin their training," he explained. "It's largely believed to be an ancient historical record of the first Necromancer. There might have been more stanzas at one point, but ol' Herbert here has been in the college for seven generations. Many impressions are faded at this point, but interestingly enough, that one remains."

"What does it mean?"

The Necromancer gave a slow grin. "That's up to you to find out."

Chapter Nine

Necromancy is known as the Frigid Art, both in the physical and metaphorical sense. It is often theorized that the casting of such magic draws not only from the emotions, but from the life force of the caster as well. You give up a part of yourself to go chasing after the dead. Only Necromancers are bold enough to accept the challenge of holding onto themselves and the dead at the same time.
- The Dying Art of Necromancy, *Author Unknown*

* * *

The Necromancer put Herbert away, struggling to get the skeleton back in the closet. Yet even with Herbert gone and the magic dismissed, Georgie couldn't think straight from shivering. At least he knew now why the Necromancer kept a fire going well into the late summer. He drew closer to the hearth, putting his boots as close to the edge as he could. He wanted to pick up the smoldering coals in his arms and shove them into his chest, where the cold seemed to sit.

There was a sudden yowl and scratching at the front door as the Void pawed at the threshold.

The Necromancer was shoving the last of Herbert's arm into the closet. "Georgie, would you get that?"

"*MEOW!*"

"Bones take you, Void, I've—" The Necromancer took one look at Georgie. "Ah."

Whatever exchange the Necromancer and his familiar had had with one another was lost on Georgie. Swiftly, the wizard opened the door, letting the sunlight pour in and the little black spot of shadow that was the Void out. In the same movement, he grabbed his black cloak from the doorway and draped it over Georgie's shoulders. The boy was tall for his age, but even the Necromancer's cloak pooled around him.

It smelled of rosemary and thyme, a welcome source of warmth and weighted comfort. The Necromancer pointed to the small pockets of herbs sewn inside. "To ward off vengeful spirits," he explained. He patted Georgie's shoulder. "Wait here."

The Necromancer bustled about his kitchen space, digging through drawers and cupboards. He took a worn wicker basket, its bristles sticking out at such uneven angles that Georgie knew at once that the Void had gotten to it first. The Necromancer shook out the cat fur, threw in whatever he'd bundled in a towel inside, looped the basket over his arm, and motioned for Georgie to follow him outside.

"Keep the cloak," he said when Georgie went to remove it. "For the moment."

Gathering the extra length in his arms, Georgie followed the Necromancer outside.

"Are we going to the tower?" asked Georgie.

The Necromancer did not stop his purposeful stride. "No. No one goes in the tower."

"The chain work you commissioned," said Georgie. "Was

that…to keep something in?"

"Perhaps it was made to keep curious children *out.*"

Georgie gulped, the awkwardly built tower suddenly taking on a new sinister light. The Necromancer led him past it, heading farther down the hill, where the trees were thin. The sun shone brightly with its afternoon light, a welcoming sight after the gloom of the Necromancer's cottage. Standing in the sun's warmth was easier. Georgie could feel the cold in his bones fade like a slinking shadow in the presence of the light.

The Necromancer sat down on the slope, facing the village below. He rested his hands on his knees and raised his face with eyes closed to bask in the sunlight.

Georgie sat next to him, slowly letting the cloak fall as his shivering subsided.

"Talking to the dead can be alarming," said the Necromancer. "I could have prepared you better." The Necromancer grabbed the wicker basket at his side. "A picnic, then." The Necromancer produced a roll of cheese, bread, and two corked flasks filled with mint tea.

They spent the next few moments attending to their meal. It was so pleasant, so normal, that Georgie found it hard to believe how eerily the day had begun. In between bites, the Necromancer continued to teach.

"No one is truly certain where the study of Necromancy stems from. It is hardly clear in the thousands of years of tomes we've collected. There are theories, of course. Theories mixed with prophecies and speculation. Some say that the art was stumbled upon by a very desperate person who then refined it. Others suggest the art has survived simply to ensure that history isn't forgotten. Regardless, there aren't many students of Necromancy. My own mentor took barely half a dozen pupils in all his wretched years."

"Your mentor?"

The Necromancer frowned. "Yes. His name was Sardis, and he was…brilliant."

Georgie sat up straight. The old wizard that his mother had helped all those years had been the Necromancer's own teacher. "Why did he choose you?"

"Because I was ruthless," said the Necromancer. "My parents raised me as such. You needed to be to keep up with such a man. I studied hard and didn't flinch at doing what was necessary. *Whatever* was necessary." The Necromancer sighed. "Still, he left without warning when I was fourteen. The last I heard of him was a note telling me he had died."

"I'm sorry," said Georgie dutifully, but his tongue itched with unspoken questions. Had his mother been the one to notify the Necromancer about his mentor's death? Had he ever met her? For once, Georgie might have found someone who would not fall into silence with grief when discussing his mother, and yet the Necromancer's tone was as final as a closed book.

"Don't be," he replied. "It's as Herbert said. Death always comes for its own."

It comes for everyone, Georgie thought to himself. *Not just Necromancers.*

"What did you do after he left?"

"I kept looking for whatever he hadn't gotten around to teaching me," said the Necromancer. "I was successful. Mostly."

"Is that what brought you to Yoricsgrave?"

"No," said the Necromancer. "It turns out my miserable mentor, Sardis, had wound up here. He left me the house, if you would believe it. It needed repair, but it had good bones." The Necromancer smiled grimly. "Besides, I like the quiet."

Georgie tilted his head. "But why have Necromancers in the first place?"

"A good question." The Necromancer hummed, wiping his mouth with a napkin. "One that students of the art have been asking the Magi Council for years. I suppose it is because it is tradition. There are a dozen stories like Herbert's. For instance, there was this one time where a Necromantic Master was asked to take part in a quest for vengeance. There was a warlord who was gathering warriors to avenge the death of his brother. With a title like 'warlord,' what else do you expect but more war and death? In the end, the old master offered to raise up the warlord's brother and save him the trouble." The Necromancer gave a crooked grin. "It didn't go over well."

"I thought you said that you couldn't raise anyone from the dead?" Georgie asked.

The Necromancer sputtered on his tea. "You can't." He beat his chest with his fist until he could catch his breath.

"But people have tried before," said Georgie.

"Never mind that," the Necromancer replied sharply. "You've spoken with your first skeleton, and now you think you're good enough to question thousands of years of theory?"

Georgie wilted in his seat. "No, sir."

"That's what I thought." The Necromancer pinched his nose with one hand and took several breaths before the shadow seemed to pass. "Hold out your hand, Georgie."

He placed an empty cicada shell into Georgie's open palm. "The simplest way to describe how Necromantic magic works is that it is like a cicada shell. It's fragile and extremely brittle to outside forces. But the impression of the creature is still there, even if the creature, the true life and soul, are gone. It is the same way with the encyclopedic skulls that we keep. Necromancy can preserve them and animate them if need be."

"Where do the souls go?"

He snorted, plucking the cicada shell from Georgie's hand. "You'll have to get a priest for that question."

"You've never wondered?"

"Oh, yes, I've wondered. But Necromancy becomes more complicated when you think about whether or not you are dooming them to a longer stretch of time away from paradise. Postponing their eternal damnation feels a little better. Ignorance is bliss in this case. Necromancers don't have the luxury to care about the soul as long as the bodies stay where I need them."

A black shadow that ignored the sun crept across the grass towards them. The Void had wandered back. Something in her mouth muffled her meow. Georgie leapt up from the ground with a shout as the Void dropped a distressingly still sparrow in front of the Necromancer.

"You wretched creature," the Necromancer said fondly. "Bringing your own lunch to the picnic, then?"

The Void rumbled like a small thundercloud, clearly pleased as she pressed herself against the Necromancer's leg.

Even the Void must do what cats do, Georgie reasoned, as his lunch pressed closer to his throat.

The Necromancer took one of the linen napkins and picked up the bird with one hand. He studied it, turning it over briefly with no hint of anything beyond studious curiosity.

"I suppose you're not really afraid of dead things," said Georgie.

"I wouldn't be in my profession for very long if I were."

Georgie stayed quiet, unsure whether or not he had failed his first lesson. He'd clearly reacted poorly to his first demonstration of Necromancy, had pressed the Necromancer so far that he'd snapped at him, and he was queasy at the sight of a dead bird. How was he supposed to bring his mother back if he couldn't last his first day?

The Necromancer noticed Georgie's long silence and beckoned him to sit back down. "Come, Georgie. It's not so bad. Necromancy is closer to life magic than one might initially think."

The Necromancer placed a slender finger on the bird's chest before he began to chant underneath his breath. *"Jokainen joka lentää ja varpunen joka putoaa."*

It was quieter than the spell to summon Herbert. A hushed breath instead of a command, speaking as softly to this creature as he might have had it been alive. He blew gently on top of the bird's head, ruffling its feathers until all became still once more. Georgie jumped as a flash of blue energy emanated from the Necromancer's palms. The light faded, but the bird didn't move.

Georgie looked at the Necromancer. "What did that—"

The Necromancer motioned back towards the bird in his hand. The crooked feet straightened with flexing, scaled toes. The wings shuddered as if remembering flight, the neck snapped back into place, and then the little bird's eyes opened once more, wide and stunned.

"There now," murmured the Necromancer, shifting it upright in his hands. "Good as new."

The bird sat up in his palm, looking back and forth. It gave a hesitant chirp, as if asking what had happened.

The Void meowed mournfully at her ruined prey.

With an alarmed squawk and fluttering wings, the sparrow took off and flew towards the tree line, as alive as it had ever been.

Georgie's mouth hung open in surprise. "But you said... I thought...?"

The Necromancer gave him a long, side-eyed look. "Don't mention this. To anyone." He stood up suddenly, throwing the flasks and remnants of the picnic back into the basket before gathering his cloak from the ground and draping it across his arm. "It's time for you to be heading home. I'm sure your mind is full enough, and it will take time to process what you've learned. I'll see you tomorrow."

Chapter Ten

Attachments are often discouraged for the Necromancer, romantic or otherwise. Due to the nature of the Necromantic arts and its reliance on emotion, such relationships are less than a strength and more like a stumbling block. We are to be as cold as our studies. Despite this, many a Necromancer has still been burnt.
  - The Dying Art of Necromancy, *Author Unknown*

* * *

The next three days followed a similar pattern. They would often begin with note-taking and a lecture, usually with Herbert animated and able to chime in. The Necromancer would provide a handful of demonstrations, often with his houseplants, or the jars filled with specimens from around his house. Then, about every two hours, the Void would scream.

The first time she did this, Georgie leapt out of his seat, splattering ink all over his notes and Herbert. The skeleton tried unsuccessfully to wipe himself off, causing the ink to drip further onto the floor beneath them.

"It's fine," said the Necromancer in a tone that suggested otherwise. "There are towels in the closet there. Use those."

With the Void still darting around his heels, screaming as if her life depended on it, the Necromancer grabbed his cloak off the rack, took a deep, calming breath, and went outside with the Void .

Georgie watched them through the dusty glass windows as the Necromancer marched briskly across the lawn directly towards the tower. He waved his hands over the door, a series of electric-blue symbols sparking across the wooden frame before they faded. The tower door opened, the inside as dark as a midnight without stars. The Necromancer and the Void both slipped inside, shutting the door firmly behind them.

"Well, that's not ominous at all," Georgie said to himself.

There was a loud clatter as Herbert, unsteadily attempting to walk, found a puddle of ink, slipped, and fell to the ground. The skeleton remained lifeless on the floor, without a single twitch to signal animation.

The Necromancer must have dropped the spell, Georgie thought as he grabbed the towels for Herbert. He picked up the surprisingly light bones, placing Herbert back on his pole before wrapping the towels around him like a toga to soak up the worst of the ink.

With Herbert taken care of, Georgie tidied up his papers and returned to his seat. But the Necromancer had not returned. Georgie leaned on his stool to look through the window again. The tower door was still shut. He waited for a few moments, taking time to look over the curious oddities in the house that surrounded him. Then, ever so slowly, Georgie got down from his seat and headed towards the bookshelves.

The memory of the sparrow, fully alive and flying, refused to leave Georgie's mind. The Necromancer had done that, with only a few muttered words of a spell. He might outwardly refuse to resurrect the dead, but he obviously knew more than he was letting on. Georgie would simply have to find the proper spell. But where does one even begin looking for an impossible miracle?

Georgie had barely touched a single spine before he heard a distant door slam shut. He ran back to his seat, slipping in the puddle of ink and falling into his chair just as the Necromancer opened the cottage door.

The Necromancer looked incredibly tired as he removed his cloak. The Void entwined herself around his ankles, purring loudly. The man bent down, scooping up the Void in his arms, and pressed his face against her fur.

"Sir?" Georgie asked.

The Necromancer looked up, the tiredness quickly covered by a wide, fake smile. "Right, then, where were we?"

* * *

The days progressed, and during the Necromancer's absences, Georgie investigated the shelves. He found very few books that he could read. Nearly everything in the library had been written in languages that he couldn't understand. After he'd noted which tomes were unhelpful for the day, the Necromancer would return, strangely drained, but eager to carry on.

Today, Georgie and the Necromancer were revitalizing the various dead houseplants.

"You seem to struggle with gaining the proper connection to your subject," said the Necromancer. Georgie had been trying for thirty minutes to get the crispy brown leaves to even turn yellow.

"It's a plant," said Georgie.

"No," the Necromancer corrected, spinning the planter around to point to the name inscribed on it. "This is Alphonse."

"You name all of your plants?" Georgie took a closer look at the various pots around him, noticing their labels for the first time. Calista, Goldie, Sven, Edward, and Dave.

"It helps grow the emotional attachment," the Necromancer replied. "A necessary component to Necromancy and the basis for reanimation." He stood up, grabbed his cloak off the coatrack, and beckoned Georgie to follow him outside.

"Animating the dead," explained the Necromancer, "is quite difficult and requires an enormous amount of energy."

"What kind of energy?" asked Georgie.

"Emotional," he replied. "Our attitudes, feelings, and emotions can be projected onto and into impressions and shells. The stronger the ties to a person's psyche, the stronger the bond to the reanimated. It's this bond that makes Necromancy difficult. For you see, no one can dismiss reanimated dead save for the Necromancer who cast the spell in the first place."

They walked a little way to a small field. Tufts of grass made it an uneven surface. There was a small fence around it, as if it were an animal pen. But as Georgie looked around, there wasn't a creature in sight.

"For our purposes today, you'll learn your first spell."

"Really?" Georgie stood up straight.

The Necromancer grinned eagerly. "As you can imagine, it's an issue, all those unstoppable undead impressions running around. Especially when you are just beginning your studies. But while you cannot send an impression to rest without the original Necromancer's release, you can stop it from rampaging around."

The Necromancer looked out towards the field, his bright,

ice-blue eyes flashing.

"Volunteers, please raise your hands."

The tufts of grass on the ground exploded. Two, three, five and then seven were torn away, each replaced with a single skeletal hand rising out of the dirt.

"Just one will do," said the Necromancer, pointing towards the closest hand. Another one joined it from beneath the earth until an entire skeleton had pulled itself out from the ground.

"If the bond is emotional, then how do you know them?" asked Georgie, taking out his notebook and quill that'd he brought from the house.

The Necromancer was silent for a long time. "They were my mentor's. Sardis. He taught me to use them, just the same as I am teaching you."

Georgie wondered when a skeleton became an object instead of a person. It was a cold, unsettled feeling that dropped over his shoulders like a wet blanket. "You don't know who they are?"

"They are whom I need them to be," he said with a bit of bite in his voice. "In this case, they are filled with great calm and patience." Georgie doubted that but kept quiet as the Necromancer's lecture continued. "Emotional projection is a particularly sore subject amongst the living. When attempted upon the dead, it robs a soul of their own intent. With enough force, or a strong will, such projection can manipulate, shaping the reanimated into less of themselves and more of whatever suits the practitioner.

"It's also this emotional connection that makes true res-urrection purely hypothetical. Current studies conjecture that in order to do so, you would need a great emotional attachment to the original soul and they to yours. By the time we Necromancers get to them, there isn't much left of that. There is only so much attachment one can have towards a person they don't know. Not to mention the grisly business of maintaining physical life such as the reapplication of muscular tissue, reintegrating the nervous system, finding the right amount of blood…" The Necromancer trailed off, suddenly aware of Georgie dutifully taking notes. The wizard reached out to pluck the quill from Georgie's hand. "As I said, hypothetical."

A very specific hypothetical, thought Georgie.

The skeleton shambled forwards, hands at its sides, as if drawn to the Necromancer like a moth to a flame. Well, Georgie supposed it very well could have been the soul of a moth. They certainly didn't seem to be anything brighter.

The Necromancer hopped over the fence, rubbing his hands together eagerly. "Now, pay attention." He made some long, swooping gestures with his arms, his eyes beginning to glow once more with the ice-blue light.

"Kuollut, älä kävele!" He muttered the incantation over and over under his breath, the light from his eyes suddenly forming in the patterns he was making with his hands. With a sharp crack, the Necromancer dropped one hand, then the other, before shoving both of them forward. The blue light shot out from his hands like lightning, hitting the skeleton in the chest. It sparked and flashed, running up each of the bones until the skeleton stopped. It was halted, frozen mid-step.

The skeleton's open mouth rattled with surprise.

The Necromancer glanced over his shoulder at Georgie, who took that as a signal to clap politely.

"The dead in question will stay this way until their connected Necromancer can come and claim them," he explained, wiping his hands off on his shirt.

"And if they don't come along?"

"Then things become more difficult," said the Necromancer. "But not impossible. You can at least shuffle the dead away to a safer place than, say, the middle of a village in the dead of night."

The Necromancer muttered under his breath again. The blue light faded from the skeleton's bones, soft and slow like thawing ice, until the skeleton in question stumbled about again.

"Now, then," said the Necromancer, clapping his own hands. "Your turn."

The Necromancer had Georgie practice the incantations over a hundred times before he even began the hand motions. The words felt like rocks in Georgie's mouth, but eventually, he managed to use the proper inflection.

The hand motions were simpler, though no less precise. Georgie's shoulders started aching on the thirtieth try, and it appeared his tutor's patience was also beginning to wane.

The Void, looking for all the world like an empty black grave staining the grass, screamed.

"Yes, yes, I know," said the Necromancer to his familiar. He nodded to Georgie. "Keep it up. I'll be back to check on you in a few moments."

Georgie dropped his hands in shock. "You're leaving me with the skeleton?"

The skeleton in question was ambling about the fenced yard. Occasionally, it would bump into the fence, changing direction, only to bump into the other side of the fence again.

"It's harmless in this state," said the Necromancer with a wry smile. He yawned. "I won't be but a moment. Shout if the skeleton gets too excited."

Georgie didn't dare ask what the Necromancer meant by that.

A moment ended up being nearly half an hour. Clearly, he'd been abandoned for the sake of the Necromancer's regular trip to the tower. Georgie's arms felt as though they would fall off, and his throat was raw from all the chanting. If the skeleton came to a stop, it was only because it had finally reached its own limit for movement.

There was a soft chuckle from over his shoulder. "Left you alone, did he?"

A woman stood behind him. Her long black hair hung in a braid and had been tossed over one shoulder. With her pale skin and deep-red-stained lips, she reminded Georgie of a fairy tale. She was dressed in gently streaming silks of purple and red, kept in place by a wide belt around her waist. She wore practical but surprisingly purple trousers that were each tucked into smart black leather boots.

She smiled at him, dimples appearing on both cheeks. "Hello, dear. I'm the Enchantress."

Georgie wiped off his sweaty palm to shake her offered hand. "Georgie."

"Enchanting to meet you, Georgie," she said, her grip gentle. "Would you like a drink? You look parched."

"Yes, ma'am. Very much so."

The Enchantress reached to her belt and handed him a full waterskin. "Freshly filled. The water inside is drawn from a spring in the mountain passage."

It was the best water he'd ever tasted. "That's amazing." Georgie regretfully wiped the remnants from his chin.

The Enchantress smiled—she smiled an awful lot—and nodded to the skeleton in the yard. "How long have they been like that?"

Georgie squinted up at the sun, dismayed to see how quickly it had moved. "An hour. Maybe more."

The woman hummed thoughtfully but said nothing. For what it was worth, she didn't seem startled by the living dead. Georgie didn't know if that was comforting or not.

"Are you here to see the Necromancer?" he asked.

The dimples in her cheeks faded. "I am."

"Have you been traveling for long?"

"Oh, no," said the Enchantress, adjusting the long purple scarf about her shoulders. "It takes very little time for me to travel. I arrived late last night from Inchante, the city beyond the mountains."

"Are you…Are you also a…magician?" Georgie asked.

There was an actual twinkle in the Enchantress's eyes as she grinned. "What gave it away? Was it the title?"

"I've never met… Well, I mean, I *have* met a magician. But just the one. You seem like a very…different kind of magician."

"Oh, quite different, I imagine."

"And insufferable." The Necromancer came up the hill like a storm cloud, stomping forward with a scowl on his face.

The light beneath the Enchantress's smile faded into caution. "I didn't know you'd taken on an apprentice."

"I didn't know that I needed your permission," the Necromancer snapped back, dragging Georgie farther away from her. "Hold out your arms," he commanded Georgie, who did as he'd been instructed. The Necromancer walked around him. "No trace of a charm spell," he murmured to himself. He stopped in front of Georgie, peering deeply into his eyes. "How long were you speaking with her?"

"They're called social skills, darling," called the woman from the fence. "It's not magic."

The Necromancer ignored her, muttering an incantation under his breath. "Stay still."

Placing both hands on Georgie's shoulders, his eyes flared with the ice-blue light as fast and bright as a falling star. There was a rush of cool breeze, sending shivers down Georgie's spine.

Finally satisfied, the Necromancer turned his attention back to the woman. "What do you want, Morgan?"

The Enchantress's smile turned sharp. "A cordial visit," she said. "You haven't written in months."

The Necromancer crossed his arms. "I've been busy."

"That never used to stop you before," said the Enchantress, earning a darker scowl. "It's a fair bit quieter here, isn't it? Compared to the city?"

"If I minded the quiet, I wouldn't work with the dead," answered the Necromancer.

"Should I leave?" asked Georgie.

The two magicians looked at him then back at each other.

"Perhaps it's best," said the Enchantress.

"No, stay," the Necromancer said at the same time.

The two magicians glared at one another for a moment, each waiting for the other to concede. But while the Enchantress's eyes were searching, the Necromancer's remained cold and unyielding.

"How… How do you two know each other?" Georgie asked.

"We went to school together," the Enchantress explained. "Many years ago." She straightened her back, pulling herself out of memory. "If you must know, I came to see you. The Council of Magi is worried, and I need your help."

The Necromancer scoffed. "*My* help? For what?"

"I need to understand why." There was weight behind her words, a silent plea to not have her explain further.

But the Necromancer didn't extend the courtesy. His scowl faded, turning into a grin. "I have an idea." He clapped Georgie on the shoulders. "How about we let my apprentice see some real magic?"

"Oh? Is this not enough?" The Enchantress gestured to the skeleton behind her.

"Mere parlor tricks. I think we are both capable of a better display than that."

"What are you suggesting?" she asked, her voice low with caution.

The Necromancer's skull-like grin returned. "I challenge you to a duel, Morgan. You and I. First to three hits concedes."

The Enchantress's never-faltering smile finally faded. "Why are you doing this, Tristan?"

If she'd meant to soothe the Necromancer, his true name had the opposite effect. The Necromancer held his hand up in the air, and with a twist of his wrist, two more sets of bony hands burst up from the ground. Two skeletons wrestled up out of the earth to join their companion, standing at a militarized attention as they awaited their next order.

"Forfeiting already?" He smirked. "You always gave up too quickly."

"Fine," the Enchantress snapped. "You will have your duel."

Chapter Eleven

Duels between magic practitioners are amongst the rarest and most spectacular displays of the various arts. For many years, the College of Magi excelled in these demonstrations, often pitting their divination students against the conjurers or the abjuration scholars against the illusionists. There was only one instance of a Necromancer being allowed to compete. No such competitions have been held ever since.

  - The Dying Art of Necromancy, *Author Unknown*

* * *

Both magicians stood on either side of the large meadow, the grass gently blowing in the wind. The Enchantress stood on the wooded side while the Necromancer had lured the skeletons from their pen out into the open space. Georgie sat a safe distance back from the center while the Void stretched out next to him, meowing mournfully.

"This is ridiculous," said the Enchantress.

"Forfeiting already, Morgan?" the Necromancer called, forcing cheer into his voice.

"Oh, shut up," she shouted back, rolling up her long, tapered sleeves.

There was a jangling sound, and Georgie jumped as Herbert the Skeleton wandered from the house towards the Necromancer. The skeleton had a couple of clothes hangers dangling from his ribs and was dragging a rug behind him.

"Is that…" The Enchantress leaned closer. "Herbert?"

Skeletons didn't recognize familiar faces, and so the lumbering undead didn't so much as turn to acknowledge her.

The Necromancer hunched his shoulders with a growl. "Enough socializing," he said, quickly pulling the clothes hangers off of the skeleton. "Call your fighters."

The Enchantress tossed her braid over one shoulder as she turned to face the woods and started to sing. Her high, almost-mournful call echoed throughout the meadow. The very breeze seemed to carry the notes far off into the distance. It was an ancient song, one that rang with greeting and the colors of sunsets. Georgie felt as though it reached into his own bones, making them hum like a tuning fork, calling him closer to her.

In the stillness that stretched between each call, Georgie heard soft footfalls.

A stag emerged from the trees bearing an impressive set of red-stained antlers with sharp points. Behind him stepped a badger with bunched, muscular shoulders and massive claws that left deep grooves in the ground beneath it.

The stag walked right up to the Enchantress, bowing his head low as if he were greeting royalty. The badger snorted its reverence, its head and body naturally low to the ground.

"Hello, friends," said the Enchantress. "I have a favor to ask of you." She paused, looking back towards the woods. "Where's the third?"

In the distance, there was a quick shuffling in the tall grass. It was approaching fast, zigzagging back and forth in the meadow. The movement stopped directly at her feet as a bright-red squirrel popped out of the tall grass.

The Enchantress laughed as she knelt down and held out her hand. "There you are! I was beginning to worry."

Unafraid, the squirrel hopped into her hand before scurrying up her arm and onto her shoulder.

Georgie turned his attention back to the Necromancer. The wizard, of all things, looked *bored*. The Necromancer stretched his arms over his head before addressing his own skeletons.

"Right, then. Anyone afraid of dying?"

The skeletons were silent.

"I thought not," said the Necromancer. "Don't hold back."

"First to three hits?" asked the Enchantress.

"First to three," the Necromancer agreed.

"May the best mage win," she said.

"Oh, I intend to," said the Necromancer. There was a loud crack as blue energy leapt off the Necromancer like lightning. It encircled the skeletons, infusing them with the strange light. The wayward dead straightened up into a more sinister stance and began marching forward towards the Enchantress.

The Enchantress raised her hands in response. Each of the animals' eyes flared the same color purple as her own. The stag reared on his hind legs with a loud call and charged.

There was a great clash of magic and bone as the stag's antlers met skeletal ribcages. The stag impaled two skeletons onto his antlers, tossing them over his head. The first skeleton fell, shattering into a pile of disjointed bones.

"First hit," said the Enchantress.

The Necromancer snarled and muttered more incantations underneath his breath. The second impaled skeleton didn't quite come free from the stag's antlers. Instead, it twisted itself into a cage of bone, wrapping itself around the stag's head and pulling it to the ground.

The badger ran forward with a loud growl. With a flash of teeth and claws, it leapt onto the skeleton, imprisoning the stag. The badger clenched its powerful jaws around the skeleton's arms, pulling at the bones until they broke away.

The red squirrel still sat on the Enchantress's shoulder. With a sharp squeak and a tug on her braid, the squirrel caught her attention. The Enchantress smiled. She reached into her own hair and removed a single silver hairpin. The red squirrel snatched the pin in its hand like a small sword and performed a few experimental swishes before placing the hairpin in its mouth and scampering down the Enchantress's arm towards the fray.

The red squirrel disappeared into the chaos as the stag continued to batter the fallen skeleton with his hooves. The badger barely dodged out of the way, a tibia of one of the skeletons still firmly clenched between its teeth. Georgie didn't see the squirrel again until he caught a glint of red fur crawling up the back of Herbert's spine.

The squirrel scaled Herbert as easily as a tree, dodging the swat of skeletal hands until it reached the base of Herbert's neck. The squirrel took the hairpin from its teeth and stabbed it in between Herbert's neck joints. With an expert twist of the hairpin, the squirrel popped Herbert's skull free from his body, where it fell to the ground. Herbert's teeth chattered angrily, snapping after the squirrel's retreating tail.

"Second hit," said the Enchantress. "Nearly there, Tristan!"

Georgie was impressed. For all the fear he'd had about Necromancers and the living dead, nature was quite adept at handling the unnatural. Georgie was sure that he shouldn't have been cheering against his mentor, but it was hard to hide his smile. But just as Georgie finished with his happy thought, the Necromancer did something unexpected.

"*Mors tua me tenet. Perdere omnes!*" He clapped his hands together, and the energy in his palms turned from a glacial blue into a deep black. The pile of bones on the ground sprang to life again, but not in its former shape. The three other skeletons broke apart, each bone flying towards the other before rising into a new monstrosity. Herbert's skeletal head rested in the center of the exaggerated ribcage. Three sets of arms jutting with spikes from shattered pieces reached towards the stag as the creature skittered forward like an enormous spider on four sets of legs.

The Enchantress's mouth fell open in horror as the Necromancer's creation swiped out with its arm towards the stag. With incredible force, the stag was thrown aside.

"First hit," called the Necromancer.

The badger let out a wail as the skeletal horror kicked it away. Only the squirrel stood in front of the Enchantress now, the hairpin wobbling in its grip.

"Second hit," said the Necromancer.

One of the hands reached towards the squirrel, grabbing it by its tail. The squirrel struggled wildly, swiping at the air with its weapon and squeaking madly. The Enchantress's face went pale as the creature raised the squirrel in the air, ready to lower it into its horrible jaws.

"Stop!" screamed Georgie. "Please stop it! You'll kill it!"

The Enchantress's head snapped towards Georgie, breaking whatever stubborn spell she'd still held. With a frustrated shout, the Enchantress fell to her knees with her head bowed.

"Enough! I yield!"

With her surrender, a burst of energy surrounded the field once more, radiating out from where she knelt. The bone creature shuddered with a chilling, deathly sigh. The deep-blue-black magic that infused the skeletal horror faded as each of the bones fell away, clattering to the ground. It let go of the squirrel. It landed hard with a scared squeak before scampering away into the grass. Four skeletons lay once again in their rest, side by side in the field, with their empty eye sockets gazing up at the sky.

With the bone creature scattered, the Enchantress got to her feet and ran towards the injured stag. Georgie followed close behind.

"There now, easy," the Enchantress murmured.

The stag groaned, lifting his head feebly off the ground. Small dots of blood coated the stag's side from the impact of the creature's spikes. The stag yelped as she pressed against his wounds.

"Georgie," said the Enchantress. "Hold his head, please."

Georgie ran to obey, kneeling by the stag's side. One of his antlers had broken off, leaving the tips more jagged than before. The stag's deep-brown eye gazed up at Georgie in pain and alarm. There was a single mote of purple light in the center of his eye, the last rapidly fading sign of the Enchantress's spell.

"It's all right," Georgie echoed. "We're here to help."

The Enchantress sang again. This song was softer, a soothing lullaby that helped stop the stag from trembling. The Enchantress reached for the stag's wounds again, but this time, her hands glowed with a calm lavender light. The wounds slowly closed, knit back together by the Enchantress's song.

The stag's breathing grew steadier as the danger passed.

"You can let go now, Georgie," she said.

He scrambled away, letting the stag get to his feet.

The Enchantress bowed low to the ground at the stag.

"Forgive me," she whispered. "I placed you in greater peril than I should have."

The stag snorted, stamping his hooves into the dirt in what seemed to be agreement. Eventually, he bowed in return. The Enchantress murmured an incantation, causing the purple mote of light to fade in the stag's eyes. The moment it was gone, the stag became wild again. He bolted away, dashing back across the meadow as fast as his healed body would carry him.

The Enchantress gave a weary sigh. "That was close."

"Where's the badger?" Georgie looked around wildly.

The Enchantress lifted her head, taking a moment to listen. "She's fine. I imagine she's already returning to her den. Badgers are made of sterner stuff. You don't need to worry about her."

"And the squirrel?" There was a flash of red fur by Georgie's feet. All that he found was a bent silver hairpin.

The Necromancer approached, holding Herbert's skull in his hands. "You held out longer than I thought you would."

The Enchantress looked pained for a moment before she straightened her spine, plastering a charming smile on once more. "You're not the only one who's a stubborn fool."

"You know better than anyone how to stop something like that," said the Necromancer quietly. "Why didn't you?"

"I grew out of my desire to wield Necromancy," she replied. "I wish you would someday." The Enchantress stopped herself. She took a deep breath through her nose before letting it out. "All I will say is this. Be careful, Tristan. You told me once that I should tell you if you were ever like him. Hear my warning now for what it is, as your friend. Please, don't get that close."

The Necromancer's lips thinned. "I think you should go, Morgan."

"You always did suffer from a lack of patience," the Enchantress replied, pulling the purple scarf from around her neck. "A gift first, for the Necromancer's apprentice."

She held her scarf out to Georgie. "It's not your color, I'm afraid, but I have a feeling you'll need this more than I will."

"Thank you," said Georgie, marveling at the soft silk in his hands.

"Keep it close," the Enchantress said, her eyes serious. "Promise me."

Georgie touched the gentle silk, running his fingertips along the embroidered runes. "I promise."

The Enchantress squeezed Georgie on the shoulder as she left, making her way down the road. She never looked back.

Chapter Twelve

Thus, the bond between Necromancer and apprentice is a gamble, a risky extent of trust as thin as a tendon and as disastrous to tear.
  - The Dying Art of Necromancy, *Author Unknown*

* * *

The tense silence was made worse by the dismissal of the skeletons. Georgie watched as each of them gathered their pieces, some to mere splinters, before returning to their burial plots. The ground consumed them as the last bit of blue energy left their open mouths with an uncanny gasp.

It wasn't until the Enchantress had disappeared below the hilltop that the Necromancer spoke again. "Were you scared?"

Georgie, still holding back his voice, only nodded in return.

"Good," he said. "Necromancy is not to be trifled with. Magic of this sort is a dark, very grim pursuit. To be a Necromancer means you face it every day. Our work doesn't become easier when you bat your eyelashes at people and use basic charms."

Georgie tugged at the scarf around his neck. "But you knew her? Before?"

"Yes," said the Necromancer. "Morgan was my classmate for

many years. I told you that my mentor didn't take on many pupils, and he didn't. It was simply the two of us for many years."

The Necromancer's gaze grew distant even as his brow furrowed. "We were tested, same as you were. For desires and emotional control. Morgan had lost her pet, whilst I had lost my parents. It's absurd that such grief would register the same, but it didn't seem to deter him. Thus, we studied together. Despite her appalling fashion sense, Morgan was…*is*, I suppose, quite talented."

Georgie could easily agree after having seen the Enchantress's power. While the Necromancer's power seemed limited to skeletons, he seemed to imply that the Enchantress had a far greater reach. It would probably be easier to charm anything beyond a skeleton. Easier to find too, or at least, Georgie hoped so. He wasn't so sure about that with the amount of them that kept popping up around Yoricsgrave.

"What happened?" he asked softly.

"She gave up." The Necromancer sniffed with disdain. "Five years of studying and suddenly, her desires changed, and she transferred to another school of magic to study. She didn't have a taste for Necromancy anymore, couldn't control herself. It had backfired on more than one occasion until eventually, she left."

"Did she ever explain why?"

The Necromancer's face twisted with pain. "She said it was better to fail than to pursue a lost cause."

Clearly, the Necromancer had taken this personally. But how could he not have? It all fell into place for Georgie. The solitary art of Necromancy was certainly lonely. Georgie knew the hurt of being abandoned. He could only imagine how painful it would be to lose your only living companion and be left with the quiet dead.

The Necromancer shook himself like a blustered buzzard. "And now she shows up here, flippant as ever, thinking she can smile her way into my good graces? Whatever she is up to here in town, it can't possibly be cordial. She's a terrible liar. That she would even consider using my own magic against me bodes ill. Very ill."

The Necromancer snapped out of his monologue, peering down his beaked nose at Georgie. "If you know what is good for you, stay away from her."

Georgie's hand went to the scarf around his neck, suddenly afraid that it would come to life and strangle him from the way the Necromancer was glaring at it. Still, he didn't toss it aside. Instead, he tucked it safely away in his pocket.

As they approached the cottage, the Void began to hiss and spit.

They'd received a visitor. One of the young priests stood at the door to the cottage, a young woman with her hair covered in a long black veil and simply dressed in solemn black. She eyed the door knocker with obvious distaste. She startled at the sound of the Void's yowling, stumbling back from the doorway.

"Sir! You've returned!" she said with a slight bow. "The Father of the Valley sends his regards."

"Does he wish to set up another funeral?" the Necromancer asked, suddenly sounding very tired.

The young woman shook her head. "No, sir. He wouldn't speak too much of it, only that it was of 'grave importance.'"

The Necromancer snorted at the emphasis. "It always is."

"Not like this, sir. The Father insisted I use those exact words, a *disturbance* of *grave* importance. He requests your presence as soon as you are able."

The Necromancer's eyes narrowed. "Very well. Return to the churchyard and tell him I'll arrive two hours after sundown, when the moon ascends."

"That long, sir?"

"This is work best left to the dark," the Necromancer replied.

The young woman bowed at her waist, taking her leave. "Thank you, sir."

"Void!" the Necromancer shouted. The cat in question meowed at his feet. "It's time." He clapped his hands together with eager glee. "Finally, a lead we can work with." He turned swiftly on his heel and ran towards the tower. "I'll need the chains, the lantern, some alchemist's fire, and my book. Don't forget the book!"

Georgie still stood on the front lawn. "Sir?"

The Necromancer froze in place. "Ah. Georgie." He leaned awkwardly against the door of the tower, trying to look as if he hadn't forgotten about him. "That's enough lessons for today, I think. You're free to go."

"Are you sure?" he asked. "Do you want help to gather up the supplies you mentioned? I can—"

"That's enough!" the Necromancer snapped, his eyes flashing blue for a moment. "I have much to do. Now go."

Georgie remembered the monstrosity that the Necromancer had summoned earlier and didn't argue.

The seed of hope that Georgie had had about his mission darkened. The Necromancer had great power, but that was far beyond any simple party tricks. If he couldn't grant life again, was he only able to further distort something in death? It was a far cry from the joyful reunion Georgie had hoped to have with his mother. The thought of bringing back the woman whom he knew as all bright smiles as a twisted creature made him shudder.

Then there was the Enchantress, a clearly powerful magician who had left the study of Necromancy because of a presumed failure. Georgie wondered what it had been, what she knew, and he desperately wished he could ask her questions. Yet if he were honest, he was afraid to know the answers.

Georgie shook his head fiercely, as if he could clear the doubt from his mind like cobwebs. No. He could still do this. He wouldn't fail his family or his mission. After all, the Necromancer had done nothing like that in front of Georgie before. The Enchantress had simply irritated him by poking at an old wound. He hoped that as long as the Enchantress stayed away, perhaps things would return to the helpful magic, like life spells, and far away from the darker aspects of Necromancy.

Chapter Thirteen

There is a point of no return for every magic practitioner. When a decision is made, a choice locked in, and a desire is finally put into motion. Nothing can stop this pursuit, save for death itself. But for the Necromancer, that moment is a welcome one.
  - The Dying Art of Necromancy, *Author Unknown*

* * *

Georgie walked into the house to find Ellory making an absolute mess of the kitchen table. She had a large spool of red twine tangled around her fingers and a dozen or so more pieces of paper scattered around her. Both the papers and Ellory jumped in alarm as Georgie shut the door behind them.

"You're home!" Ellory squeaked, scrambling to gather up her papers and stuff them into her open notebook.

Georgie set his notebook and bag by the door. "He ended our lessons early," he explained. "What are you doing?"

His cousin gave up trying to untangle the twine and simply threw it into her bag on the table. "Cleaning." She scowled. "Like I'm supposed to."

Ellory might not have liked Georgie keeping secrets, but he

would let her have her own. Aunt Elisa had sent Ellory over to keep her out of trouble but no ten-year-old wanted to clean a house as large as this one.

"Would you like some help?" he offered. "We can talk about my lessons while we tidy up."

For the rest of the afternoon, Georgie helped Ellory about the house. He swept the stairs while Ellory dusted every nook of the large house. They brought in the wash from the laundry line. Together, they made a game with the sheets by seeing how hard they could run and bump into each other when folding end to end. In between the sneezing from the dust and the laughter of their game, he told her all about the wizards' duel.

"The Enchantress? I've seen her around town," said Ellory. "Pretty woman with black hair and lots of purple?"

"That's the one," said Georgie, his fingers drifting into his pocket towards her scarf.

"She was definitely asking questions," said Ellory. "I would know! I tried to listen in a few times, but then the church bells rang, and I knew Mum would be mad if I was late. Do you think they're rivals?"

"I think they were friendly at one point," said Georgie. "Now, I'm not so certain. The Necromancer doesn't seem to care for her much anymore. But she certainly is powerful."

Ellory tapped her pencil on her chin. "I wonder what she's doing here, then."

Georgie shrugged. "Whatever it is, the Necromancer warned me to stay away."

Despite how thin the information was, Ellory soaked it all in as eagerly as a sponge. She perched on the kitchen table, leaning over her tattered notebook to write whatever she'd learned in the margins of the crowded pages.

"Have you figured out Herbert's riddle yet?" she asked.

Georgie blinked. He'd been so busy digging through the library for information that he'd forgotten all about it. But Ellory wasn't deterred by his silence and continued on. "I think it has something to do with the giants. Or at least, that's a big clue. *Falling where they once slept. Walls of bone became stone.*"

It was a good guess. Yoricsgrave was alive with giant folklore. They were kin to them in a way and often heralded as the reason all the village folk grew tall. There was something in the soil, or the water, that made everything grow large. Even the Strands Festival boasted a larger-than-life vegetable competition each year.

"You're going to figure it all out before I am, aren't you?" he asked with a grin.

"Mum says that if I work hard enough, I might be able to go to college someday," said Ellory with a wistful look in her eyes. "There are a dozen different ones, but I'm really interested in the ones that are in the big cities. Maybe I'll even go to the same college the Necromancer studied at!"

His cousin's place wasn't scrubbing houses. She belonged in the big cities, exploring and finding out new discoveries that would change the world. She was bright and clever. Just as her father had always been rumored to be.

Eventually, the Blacksmith came inside from the forge. He nodded to them both, casting a careful eye over the house. "Good work."

"Thank you, sir," said Ellory, her smile fading as her weariness grew.

"Did you dust the mantel?" asked the Blacksmith.

"Yes, sir."

The Blacksmith crossed his arms. "Check it again."

"But I thought I—"

"Go look," he ordered.

Ellory stood up from the table, grabbing a dust rag with a quizzical look on her face as she went over. She picked up a small parcel wrapped in paper and twine. The Blacksmith nodded for her to open it. When her back was turned, he winked at Georgie.

Ellory's delighted shriek was most certainly heard from across the village. "It's beautiful!" She held up a fine leather-bound notebook. Intricate leaves had been pressed into the design, with a touch of gold marking its value. A single green silk ribbon lay inside, another wrapping to the gift of clean, blank paper.

"The shopkeeper told me you'd been after it," the Blacksmith explained with a laugh as Ellory marveled over it. "Now you can stop pestering him."

She held it to her chest. "Thank you, Uncle."

"You're welcome, Ellory." The Blacksmith went to wash his hands but paused at the stovetop. "I thought I told you not to bother cleaning this." The stovetop sparkled, every single piece of debris carefully scrubbed away.

Ellory hid her grin behind her new notebook. "Mum said you'd say that. She also told me to tell you that if I didn't, she'd have to charge you extra on the next round."

The Blacksmith made a noise in his chest. "Very well, then."

Georgie's father made dinner for them that night, dismissing each and every offer of help. It was a simple meal of cold-cut sausage, fresh tomato slices, and the last of the cheese. The Blacksmith wasn't a cook, but it was a grand meal all the same.

"How's your mother getting on?" asked the Blacksmith as the meal was winding down.

"Mum's been breaking her back over those linens," said Ellory, still reverently focused on her notebook. "Mrs. Havershem told her yesterday that the date of the wedding was moved up, so she needs them even sooner now."

"*What?*" The Blacksmith turned his head sharply.

Ellory clapped her hands over her mouth. "I wasn't supposed to tell." The Blacksmith waited until she relented. "She's been working long hours. I don't think she sleeps much."

Something behind the Blacksmith's eyes flared like a rekindled forge. "Georgie, pack up the rest of this for your aunt. I'll be back." He went upstairs with footsteps as heavy as thunder.

Ellory winced. "Is he mad at me?"

Georgie shook his head. "No. I think he's mad at Mrs. Havershem."

The Blacksmith came back down the stairs with a small but very full pouch of coin. He dropped it in front of Ellory. "Take this to your mother. Tell her to buy off the old bat, or send for whatever she wants from the city. It should be more than enough."

Ellory's eyes went wide. "But that's… She wouldn't…"

"If she has any complaints, she can bring them to me."

There was a long pause. Ellory was grateful, Georgie was sure of it. But even he knew how stubborn Aunt Elisa could be.

"You're right," said the Blacksmith with a sigh. "It's time I talked with your mother, anyway. I'll go to her." He took back the coin purse and headed to the door. "Stay here at the house tonight, Ellory. It's getting late."

The sun was barely setting, but the Blacksmith's mood left little room for argument.

"She won't listen," Ellory warned. "You know that."

The Blacksmith squared his shoulders. "Then I shall have

to be convincing." With a sigh and a nod to himself, he went outside into the fading evening hours.

"What was that all about?" asked Georgie, baffled by the sudden change in his father.

Ellory watched the Blacksmith walk farther down the road, her lips slowly turning into a half-smile. "I have an idea." She turned back to Georgie. "You never did tell me why the Necromancer sent you home early."

"Oh. One of the priests sent word that they wanted to see him tonight," Georgie explained. "Something about needing him back at the graveyard."

Ellory's eyes lit up. Georgie knew that look.

"No. No, Ellory. We can't! If he even—"

But his cousin had already darted off to gather supplies.

Chapter Fourteen

Emotions, like magic, are tricky things. They can be fleeting or they can remain, becoming stronger and more potent to those around them. To wield magic, one must be sensitive to such emotions. However, there is a balance. If a Necromancer is not careful, their intentions can be swept away by emotions as if caught up in a riptide. Often to disastrous results. To my greatest shame, I have experienced this firsthand.

  - The Dying Art of Necromancy, *Author Unknown.*

* * *

Within record time, Ellory had scrounged up two oilskins, a small lantern, and the determination to go to the graveyard, regardless of whatever logic and valid protests Georgie might come up with.

"Mum says that I'm not supposed to wander off alone anymore," she explained as Georgie struggled to keep up with her on the cobblestone path. "Besides, you're studying with a Necromancer. Surely, if anything were to happen, you'd be able to help."

Georgie failed to see how history lessons from a skull would prove useful in this situation but kept quiet lest the dead heard and got any ideas. "We shouldn't be here, Ellory. If he'd wanted me to come, he'd have told me."

"Oh, hush, you're studying!" Ellory gave a wink. "Think of it as extra credit."

"Extra trouble," Georgie grumbled. "What if Da—"

Ellory snorted. "He and Mum are busy. Trust me. He won't even notice."

"Do you know something?"

"I have a theory," she said cryptically. "But more on that later. We have to hurry!"

They approached the graveyard from the top of the hill where Ellory had discovered a break in the wall. The trees offered them cover as they crawled through and slunk their way towards the chapel. The sun had set long ago, but even the moonlight faded, covering itself with clouds like a mourning veil.

Ellory found a hiding spot in the shadows of the chapel, tucked beneath several prickly rose bushes. The thorns were less than inviting, poking and prodding Georgie as he crawled behind them.

The next hour was a miserable one. Ellory refused to answer further questions or complaints. Instead, she shushed him and sat forward with her eyes locked on to the path in front of the chapel. The wind turned cold, and Georgie felt his desire to speak fade amid his growing nerves.

Finally, there was the jingling sound of keys as the Necromancer approached the chapel door. His lithe frame looked like a stretched shadow, with his cloak and hood draping about his shoulders and face. In his hand, he carried a lantern. The fire inside was a cool but vibrant blue. A smaller shadow circled about his feet. The Void stayed close beside him.

Georgie jumped as the door to the chapel creaked open. Ellory clamped her hand down on his shoulder, shooting him a last warning glance.

The Priest stood in the doorway, his pale, wrinkled face and bald head gleaming in the lantern light. The holy man's white church robes were a stark contrast to the shadow of death in front of him. "Thank you for coming," he said. "Would you like to come in?"

The Necromancer took a single step backwards. "No, thank you. The crypts in your chapel will not be as welcoming."

"Ah, you're right," said the Priest with a nod. "Don't want to add to our trouble, do we? Wait here."

When the Priest emerged again, his white robes were covered with a brown cloak, and he held his own lantern, lit with the familiar orange-and-red flame.

"Your messenger said you needed me for a matter of grave importance," said the Necromancer.

"Indeed. Our groundskeeper has reported a number of strange occurrences," said the Priest as he and the Necromancer walked away.

Ellory huffed but sprang to her feet, flitting between gravestones to keep up with them. Georgie was less graceful, but following Ellory's lead seemed to work well enough.

"For how long?" asked the Necromancer.

"The last week," answered the Priest. "Groundskeeper Bron doesn't startle easily on these lands. But with the latest happenings, he's growing nervous."

The Priest led the Necromancer towards the oldest part of the graveyard. Deep in the center lay a hilltop with various gravesites. The tombstones they passed were worn, many barely legible. But Georgie could still feel the grooves of script, ancient and unfamiliar, as he and Ellory hid behind the stones.

There was another lantern up ahead, this one held by a gruff man in his mid-fifties. His arms were crossed as he waited, displaying the muscle he'd earned after years of gravedigging. His demeanor changed as the Priest and Necromancer approached. He snatched the worn cap off his head and gave an awkward bow to the Necromancer.

"Good evening, Groundskeeper," said the Necromancer. "What is the problem that I was summoned for?"

The Groundskeeper ducked his head, suddenly shy as he gestured to the gravestone in front of him. He reached down, grabbing hold of a long length of burlap that covered the dirt in front of the gravesite.

Half of a skeleton lay sticking out from the mud. Its bony hands had left claw marks on the earth above it. One hand was raised out in front while its empty face stared up at the sky.

"This is Master Barron, sir. The second son of the original Baron from Olangrad, buried in 1543. He—"

The Necromancer cleared his throat.

Groundskeeper Bron took the hint. "Begging your pardon, sir, but Master Barron here crawled up six feet from underground." He clutched his hat nervously between his hands. "I've never seen anything like it. But I checked the others, and there were more of the same. Half out of their coffins, burrowing upwards as if they've been called too. There's the entire Arvol family, six cousins of the Corkshires, and even..."

Georgie could barely make out the Necromancer's eyes in the dark. Only the fluttering sparks of the blue lantern light showed any sign of them at all.

"Who else knows about this?" he asked softly.

"No one else, sir," replied the Groundskeeper.

"We thought it best not to disturb as much as possible," said the Priest. "Even if it meant decades-long grief."

"Can you sort it to rights, sir?" asked the Groundskeeper.

The Necromancer crouched down next to the skeleton, waving his hand over the face once. *"Redire ad mortem."* The blue light sparked from his fingertips into the eye sockets of the skeleton. It shook and shuddered and, with a sigh, sank back beneath the ground as if it were water.

"Residual Necromantic energy," he said as he stood, wiping the dirt from his hands.

The Void gave a low meow.

"Residual?" asked Groundskeeper Bron.

"It's an uncommon and sloppy effect amongst the highly trained magic practitioners," explained the Necromancer. "Power bleeds out like a contained smoke. The dead that are caught within the radius react as a plant would to the movement of the sun."

"Who would do such a thing?"

"I doubt whoever it is is even aware that it is happening," the Necromancer said firmly. "They're simply shedding, like this lantern sheds its light. Not enough to set everything aflame, but powerful enough to draw the dead."

"Wow," Ellory breathed.

Georgie gulped. He'd seen the pinned butterflies in the Necromancer's cottage that fluttered when he walked by, but what sort of creature would have enough residual magic to make the dead crawl out from their own graves?

"This is happening only to the oldest graves?" asked the Necromancer.

"Correct," affirmed the Priest. "The seals on the others still hold."

"I'll admit, sir, I thought you mad when you waltzed in here seven years ago and wanted to perform such magics," said the Groundskeeper. "Now I wish I'd let you do it sooner."

The Necromancer didn't reply, taking up his lantern once more. "I'll search the grounds," he said. "Put whatever else is disturbed back to its rest."

"Do you…?" It was the Priest's turn to speak nervously. "Do you need assistance?"

The Necromancer's smile cut across the darkness of his face like a sickle moon. "No. Come along, Void."

The cat's eyes began to glow with the same blue light as the lantern. With a quick shake of her fur, the Void bounded forward, leading the Necromancer away.

Georgie tugged on Ellory's sleeve. "Can we go now? Please?"

Ellory nodded. "Yeah, we can go."

* * *

"Residual Necromantic energy," Ellory squeaked once they were far away. "That's amazing!"

They sat next to Adelaide's grave, catching their breaths before they headed home. The familiar gravestone shone like a beacon of light on top of the hill. The clouds had parted for the moment, reflecting off the marble as strongly as if it were a lighthouse itself.

"I thought he almost saw us for a moment there," said Ellory, still buzzing with excitement. "Wish I had a light. I have so much I need to write down. Do you think you can help me remember?"

Georgie let Ellory ask questions to the air as he rested.

The phrase from Adelaide's grave rang in his mind. *'In Rest Undisturbed.'*

The Necromancer was sealing graves to prevent errant Necromantic magic. That explained what the Necromancer had done to Oldman Woodsman's coffin. But why would he have needed to do such a thing? Even more so, why had he known to do so?

Suddenly, the stone against Georgie's back grew cold, jolting through his bones as swift and as merciless as it had that first day with the Necromancer.

Ellory noticed. "What's the matter?"

Georgie stood, pulling Ellory up with him. There was an unfamiliar scent on the wind, rot and overturned earth. He heard footfalls, soft at first, a slow shambling coming up behind them, only noticeable by the faint clinking of chains and whistling wind through tattered cloth.

"Ellory," whispered Georgie. "Something's here."

Chapter Fifteen

To add flesh and bone to that which has passed only reveals the capacity and monstrousness of such an act. That our own imaginations, whether desperately innocent or malevolently possessive, can create a being that isn't wholly human.
 - The Dying Art of Necromancy, *Author Unknown*

* * *

The clouds above parted, shining with clarifying light into the darkness behind them.

Something—no, *someone* was walking towards them. The figure had slow and halting steps, slumped over to one side as it dragged one arm behind itself. It was nearly six feet tall and so slender, it seemed to be able to slip through the moonbeams to stay in the shadows below. When it realized that the children had seen it, it raised its arms towards them with grasping hands.

Georgie grabbed Ellory's arm. "Run!" Together, they scrambled down the hill, leaning forward as if the momentum would help them pick up speed.

The Creature gave chase.

Georgie's guilt screamed at him with each step. He should

never have allowed Ellory to come here. She was in danger, and it was his fault. Nevertheless, they ran as fast as frightened deer, leaping over crumbling gravestones to anywhere far away from the horror that followed them.

There, in the distance, Georgie saw a wisp of blue lantern light.

The Necromancer! He was still here! If anyone could stop this creature, it would be he.

Georgie slammed to a halt. Ellory slammed against his back, shouting out in alarm.

If the Necromancer found out that he was here, what would the man do? Surely he would be angry. Georgie had broken one of the rules. The Necromancer could refuse to tutor Georgie. The boy would never be able to bring his mother back.

"This way!" Ellory took the lead, grabbing Georgie and pulling him in a new direction.

The clouds were thinning now, leaving strips of moonlight to drift across the graveyard. With their own pulses pounding in their ears, they came to a familiar hill. She'd led them to the oldest gravestones, back where the Necromancer had returned the unearthed skeleton to its rest.

The ground shifted beneath Georgie's feet, roiling beneath him like an ocean wave as the immense cold at his back grew as sharp as ice.

"Up here!" Ellory said, motioning him towards the large mausoleum at the top of the hill.

The footfalls were approaching fast. The Creature was getting closer.

And the oldest graves were still unsealed.

The shifting ground exploded beside them as a skeletal hand reached out from the earth. Only the cold alone froze the screams in their throats as another gravesite shifted, revealing an open-mouthed skull with dirt falling from its empty eye sockets as it rose from the ground.

They kept running, dodging dirt, rocks, and bone. More skeletal hands reached upwards towards them, scratching and clawing towards the unnatural cold of the Creature behind them like moths to a flame.

Georgie cried out as he fell, shouting even as the surrounding bones scrambled to take hold. Ellory's solid grip gone, he made it to his feet by sheer terror alone.

"Quick! In here!" Ellory was waiting for him at the mausoleum next to a pitch-black open doorway.

The Creature gave a loud, mournful and breathy wail.

They ran headlong into the darkness of the mausoleum, both shoving their shoulders against the large door to seal it shut. In the door's gap, for a split second, Georgie saw the Creature, a shambling figure, moving fast up the hill, with two skeletons crawling up out of their graves behind him.

Georgie and Ellory shut the door, pressing both their backs to it. The only sound was their labored breathing as both of them desperately tried to keep quiet.

The footsteps were still outside. The jangling of chains creaked to a stop.

Silence. Drifts of cold mist began flowing from underneath the door. Then an ever-so-polite knock on the door sounded above their heads.

"Giant's teeth," Ellory swore, her voice cracking with fear.

They heard footfalls again, retreating this time. A pause and then they quickened, heading straight towards them as if to barrel through the door.

The familiar yowl of a cat broke the silence. The cold snapped as a lightning bolt cracked outside. The Creature gave another mournful cry, bellowing like a wounded animal before changing its course to flee.

Georgie could barely hold back his sob of relief as he heard the Necromancer muttering to himself outside.

"What a mess," said the Necromancer.

The Void meowed in response and scratched at the door.

Of course that spiteful cat would try to betray Georgie now.

"Come away from there, Void," called the Necromancer. "If we hurry, we might be able to catch him."

The Void kept scratching, putting her little black dagger paws beneath the door as if she were trying to pull it open. "Meow!"

"There's no one in there," said the Necromancer. "We need to leave. Now."

The Void gave an irritated yowl back at him but finally left the door. With a loud sigh and a string of incantations and cursing, the sounds of the Necromancer and his familiar faded into the dark.

But there was still one problem.

"Ellory?" Georgie asked, reaching in the dark for her hand. "Where are we?"

"Yoric's crypt," Ellory answered upon catching her breath.

Georgie's stomach dropped in despair.

The oldest and largest standing structure of the graveyard, the onyx stone mausoleum was a mystery. No one in the village truly knew who had been buried here, but the name Yoricsgrave was as old as the crypt. The village had sprung up around it. Most simply assumed someone named Yoric had been buried here a long, long time ago.

In the daylight hours, the structure seemed to absorb the light and always felt cold whenever anyone had the misfortune of walking by it. Few were buried nearby, and the caretakers avoided it when they could, leaving nature to run its course. It was a common enough dare amongst the rest of the village children to 'spend the night at Yoric's crypt.' Georgie never believed those who bragged about their success, and he kept away from any vicious children who would try to thrust such a dare on him.

But Ellory was different.

"How did we even get in here?"

There was a scratching sound next to him, then a flare of light as Ellory lit a long matchstick. She held it like a torch above their heads. "I got bored at the Woodsman's funeral and went exploring. I've been here a couple of times, but that day, I noticed something." Her grin looked sinister in the low light. "It was unlocked."

"So we can get out?"

"I think so." She climbed to her feet. "There's not exactly a door handle on this side, but I have this." She handed Georgie the matchstick torch before rifling through her bag again to produce a crowbar. Georgie's mouth fell open as Ellory swung in around in triumph. "Always come prepared!"

"We need to get home." He had to get Ellory away from here.

"We will," said Ellory, seemingly unscathed by the horror that had just happened. "But don't you want to look around?"

"No!" Georgie exclaimed, even as she lit another match. He wanted to go home, find every blanket in the house, and burrow beneath them forever. He'd make the largest pot of ginger root tea that he could to burn away the last remnants of the cold. Even if it clung more to his memory than his skin.

"I think that is the same Creature that got Oldman Woodsman," said Ellory. "It has to be! It's the only thing that the

Woodsman wouldn't have expected. Some undead, horrible thing with enough magic on it to raise the dead!" Ellory gave a happy shriek. "This is so amazing!"

Georgie instantly remembered the skeleton monstrosity that the Necromancer had conjured and gulped. That certainly fit the Creature that he had just seen. But could something like that really be alive and walking around on its own? And if the Necromancer wasn't in control of it, then who was?

With Ellory's torch of matchsticks growing brighter, it became apparent that the inside of the crypt was ancient and larger than the outside seemed to suggest. In the center lay a slab of pure obsidian, glittering underneath the firelight to reveal an engraving at the top.

"There are runes here," said Ellory. "Georgie, come read this."

He wasn't eager to get any closer, but knowing that his cousin wouldn't leave until her curiosity was satisfied, he tiptoed over to her side.

"Can you read what it says?" she asked, bringing her torch closer.

He could. "It's a name. Kaspar Cynward. That's all it says."

In the light, their reflections distorted across the obsidian. "That sounds almost…normal," said Ellory, narrowing her eyes in suspicion. "And if this is Kaspar, then who's Yoric?"

"Maybe the legends are wrong," said Georgie. He dearly hoped they were. "Old stories change over time."

"Stories like these?" Ellory raised her torch high into the air, revealing the carvings along the wall.

The carvings were remarkably well preserved. Georgie had to admit that it hadn't been disturbed for a long time. There was a man, presumed to be Kaspar, on the wall directly behind the coffin. A thin-faced man with a short beard spread his arms wide. Thin tendrils were carved away from his hands like sunbeams.

Ellory drew closer. "Wonder what this could—" Suddenly, she tripped and screamed.

"ELLORY!" Georgie ran.

"I'm fine, I'm fine," she said, her voice decidedly more trembling than it had been moments before. She sat in a pool of discarded and frayed rope. "I thought it might have been something else. What are these even doing here, anyway?"

Georgie didn't know how many more scares his heart could take. "We need to go."

"Yeah," Ellory finally agreed. She passed her torch off to Georgie in favor of her crowbar. "Sorry for bothering you, Mr. Cynward."

* * *

They didn't dare speak a word again until they were safely back at the house.

"Do you think the Enchantress released something?" asked Georgie. They were finally curled up underneath their blankets. By some unspoken agreement, Ellory was spending the night in Georgie's room.

Ellory pondered this. "Why would she do that?"

"To keep him distracted, maybe. I'm not sure, but they were students together, so she knows some Necromancy… Maybe she tried something and it went wrong. She did ask him for help. She said she needed to understand why."

The Necromancer had implied that she was emotional and flighty. Certainly, such a person would struggle to carry Necromantic energy. Perhaps the Enchantress wasn't as in control as she thought. It could explain why the Necromancer had been so angry to see her.

"That, I don't know," said Ellory. "But I'll look—" She interrupted herself with a loud yawn. "Tomorrow. I'll look tomorrow."

Georgie didn't sleep well. His legs still felt the need to run away, and he swore he could still hear the Creature's wail on the wind. In the morning, he couldn't remember if he'd slept at all. Georgie and Ellory both sat at the kitchen table, staring bleary-eyed at the oatmeal in front of them. The thick mud coating his shoes at the door and the tiredness deep in his bones told him that the previous night had indeed happened.

They both winced as the Blacksmith came in through the front door, letting in long rays of bright sunlight.

"Morning, Georgie," he said with a bright smile. "Ellory." He ruffled Georgie's hair and went to the stove, whistling.

"Have you been out all night?" Georgie asked. He'd been too exhausted to notice until now.

The Blacksmith ducked his head, his voice sheepish and soft. "I went to talk to Elisa and…"

Ellory snorted into her tea, sputtering until she had to place her cup down.

Georgie could feel his panic rising. His father had been out all night, and Georgie hadn't noticed. It had been ages since he'd done that. Usually, Georgie could tell when his father was thinking about wandering away, but last night, he had seemed fine. Confused and tired, he got up and reached for the kettle in his father's hands. "Here, let me."

"It's all right, son," said the Blacksmith. "I thought you'd be up at the wizard's house by now."

Georgie's head whipped around towards the cuckoo clock on

the wall, where the hands of the clock lingered judgmentally around noon.

"You're late!" Ellory shouted as Georgie grabbed his muddy boots, threw on whatever shirt smelled the least appalling, and haphazardly dashed out the door.

Chapter Sixteen

The intentions of those who wish to pursue magic are incredibly important. These cannot be hidden, despite how deeply one may repress their emotions.

*The hues of magical intent** are:*

** Purple - a royal color, often a symbol of importance*

** Blue - calm but also control. Deeper variants of this can denote struggle within its caster.*

** Green - seen most often in those who work with nature. Growth and life energy.*

** Yellow - hard to determine; seen often in the earliest magical exercises.*

** Ruby Red - the purest form of love and self-sacrifice. Very rare. The heart of such a person must be protected at all costs.*

Such was my own when I began my lessons, but I am certain that it is very different now.

*** The College of Magi recognizes that there are several wizards who succeed in this study despite being color blind or fully without sight. They are currently developing their own theories of accessibility for future magic practitioners.*

\- The Dying Art of Necromancy, *Author Unknown*

* * *

The sun was bright today with a gentle, cool breeze, a stark and welcome contrast to the terrifying night from before. As Georgie ran, his thoughts ran too. Giant's teeth, he was tired. But he didn't want to disappoint the Necromancer. If he didn't show up, would the Necromancer know that he'd been at the graveyard?

More than that, his father was getting worse. First, his distance at the funeral. Then there'd been the long hours at the forge. Now, he was leaving again with little explanation. How had things gotten so bad so quickly? Georgie had to go to make things right.

Georgie was breathing hard when he reached the peak of the hill where the Necromancer's house sat. He rubbed at his eyes and slapped at his cheeks to wake himself up before knocking on the door.

"Go away!" the Necromancer yelled from inside the house.

"Sir?" he called, knocking once more.

"I told you, I'm not in the mood for your *enchanting* company. Now go away!"

There was a loud yowl from the Void, some muttered cursing, and then the unbolting of no less than half a dozen locks before the door opened.

The Necromancer looked terrible.

Georgie had often heard the phrase 'like death warmed over,' but it was different seeing it on a person. The deep, dark circles beneath the Necromancer's eyes betrayed his own lack of sleep and gave his face a more skeletal image. His hair was scattered to one side, and his shoulders were slumped forward with weariness. Even the Void, curling once more around the

Necromancer's ankles, looked more decrepit in the morning light.

He blinked slowly as recognition dawned on him. "Georgie?"

Georgie forgot about his own weariness in an instant. "Are you all right, sir?"

The Necromancer managed enough energy to lift a pale brow. "No." He rubbed his hands down his face. "I had a long night. I'm afraid I'm not up to teaching today." He shut the door.

"Wait!" Georgie grabbed the handle. "Do you need help?" Surprising himself, Georgie didn't wait for an answer. He slipped past the Necromancer inside the house.

Georgie felt it at first. There was a tension in the air, crackling over his skin like the air before a lightning strike. The fire still roared, but the light barely reached past the sofa. The butterflies were fluttering anxiously in their boxes, beating their wings against the glass and pins as they tried to get away, pulsing with residual Necromantic energy.

It was worse than Georgie had thought. "Have you eaten anything?"

"No," snapped the Necromancer, slamming the door behind him.

Georgie watched as the plants in their pots curled away from the Necromancer's approaching shadow. "Did you have company earlier?"

"I was rudely awakened after a hard night by someone wanting to have a lovely chat, yes," said the Necromancer. "Blasted woman doesn't know when to keep her mouth shut or leave well enough alone." He slumped down in his chair with an angry snarl on his lips.

"Maybe she's concerned about you?"

"Ha!" The fire leapt up with the Necromancer's bitter laugh.

"Not a chance."

It frightened Georgie to see the Necromancer this way, irritated and flammable. If there were monsters about, they would need him in better shape. He wished he'd gotten here before the Enchantress. She appeared to mean well, or perhaps she had been in her own distress. Regardless, she'd clearly made him angry at the worst time.

There was a scratching sound from inside the closet door. *"But Death-Weaver's victory was sundered..."*

"Is that Herbert?" Georgie asked.

A breathy voice echoed from inside. *"The man lies there still to this day, never to atone."*

The Necromancer glared at the door. "I told you, bonehead. Be quiet!"

"The lesson here, dear Necromancer, is that death always comes for its own..."

"I said, *silentium cadaver*," the Necromancer shouted again, thrusting his hand out towards the door. A bolt of dark-blue electric energy leapt from his hand and landed on the door, spreading out like a spider's web across it.

Herbert did not speak again.

"You should go, Georgie," said the Necromancer.

But his feet refused to move. "It's fine," Georgie said, swallowing the fear stuck in his throat. "I used to do this for my da all the time. It's not a problem. Really."

Before the Necromancer could protest again, Georgie rolled up his sleeves, a learned habit from Aunt Elisa, and got to work. He shook off the cat hair from a crumpled quilt and wrapped it around the Necromancer's shoulders. The Necromancer would need food and tea. Everything was better with tea, but maybe some water first. What about the Void? He'd never seen the cat actually eat and assumed she somehow simply absorbed the light for sustenance.

The area of the cottage that might have been a kitchen lay in disarray. Georgie forced a wide smile as he worked, dashing around the cottage from one task to the next to hide his own trembling and weary legs.

"Did you know that my mother used to help your old mentor?" Georgie asked. "I bet she did the same thing for him."

The Necromancer gave a huff but stayed quiet beneath his blanket.

"I think you would like her, or at least, you would have," he continued, stumbling over the past tense. "She had auburn hair, like mine. She liked books and animals. She might have even been able to charm the Void."

The words flowed out of Georgie, anxious and eager. If he could only convey how special his mother was, maybe the Necromancer would understand why he needed to bring her back. Perhaps Georgie could convince the Necromancer to take better care of himself if he knew that someone needed him. Because Georgie did.

He needed the Necromancer to be whole and well to bring his mother back. Perhaps, if he could care enough for the Necromancer, he might do so in return. He was in a terrible state now, but surely, underneath it all was a heart. The Necromancer had to know that the reason Georgie so desperately needed his mother back was so that someone could finally care for *him*.

By the end of an hour, the Necromancer had a steaming cup of chamomile tea in his hands. The Void was resting comfortably on his lap, her small belly full of sardines. The crumbs of a sandwich were all that remained on the plate next to him.

"How are you feeling?" Georgie sat on the edge of the chair

across from the Necromancer, watching him closely for signs of improvement.

"This is…nice," said the Necromancer. "Thank you."

The surrounding cottage seemed to echo Georgie's sigh of relief. "Of course."

The Necromancer's chin drooped towards his chest, signaling an oncoming nap. Georgie gathered the teacup and plate from in front of him before putting it away in the sink. The Necromancer snorted in his sleep but didn't wake. The Void watched Georgie from the Necromancer's lap, slowly blinking her large green eyes.

* * *

Georgie shut the door behind him, slumping forward against it as his own forgotten weariness reappeared. One last walk down the hillside and then he could sleep. As he pushed himself upright, Georgie felt a sharp and sudden chill running down his spine like cold water.

But there was nothing behind him except for the tower. The tower sat gloomily in the corner, somehow resisting the bright daylight and casting a dark shadow over the house. It had the look of a weatherworn tombstone, silent and judgmental.

The wind picked up, and the tower door creaked open with a mournful sigh.

The Necromancer must have left it unlocked, he thought. Or had the Enchantress weaseled her way inside?

Georgie cast a glance at the cottage door behind him. He knew the tower was off limits. But he also knew that if anyone else were to find it this way, it might make the Necromancer far angrier.

He would have to set it right before he could leave. Georgie wiped his clammy hands on his pants as he approached.

There didn't appear to be any windows in the tower. Instead, what little light there was filtered through the gaps in the stone and the broken shingles on the ceiling. It was a simple round room, perhaps twelve feet all the way around. There was a chair in the center of the room, unadorned and plain. The only other furniture inside was a cluttered table on the side of the tower closest to the door.

There didn't seem to be much that had been disturbed here. Merely an unlocked door and a cluttered desk. Georgie's sigh of relief froze in front of him. The whole tower felt like an icebox, causing his teeth to chatter in his skull.

Right, then. No time to linger. There wasn't much left to be done, but a little tidying up couldn't hurt. He'd just stepped towards the desk when his foot hit something wet and sticky. He lifted his shoe, revealing the sole stained black. There was an ink spill drying from the night before. Georgie grabbed a rag from the table, wiped the bottom of his shoe, and propped up the now-empty inkwell back onto the desk.

Luckily, the ink had damaged none of the papers strewn about the desk. It was usually cluttered, but Georgie noticed a certain frantic energy to it. Long lines of hasty scribbling lay across the parchment, with sketches and notes.

Escaped again. But how? The wards aren't holding. I need something older. Something different or new. Something the Creature does not know of.

The Necromancer hadn't been successful against the Creature, then. It was a sobering thought. Georgie made a mental note to warn Ellory off of any further night escapades. Quietly, he gathered up the papers into a neat stack, setting them safely away from the rest of the ink and quills.

Georgie jumped, startled by an ink sketch of a skull leering out at him. *The Dying Art of Necromancy*. The deep-black grimoire lay open, with the black satin ribbon running across the pages and mirroring the ink stain on the floor.

He hadn't seen the tome since his first day at the cottage. He reached for it, flipping through the faded parchment to earlier pages. Georgie was surprised to discover that he could read it all. Whereas the other tomes were a mix of various languages and runes, this appeared to be more of a journal. Sketches, runes, and lists dotted the pages in a tidy script.

Perhaps this was what he'd been searching for all along.

"MEOW!"

Georgie shut the tome, leaping nearly out of his skin at the loud yowl behind him.

The Void stood in the doorway, her tail twitching curiously.

"Giant's bones, Void. You scared me," said Georgie, reaching for his chest to keep his wildly beating heart within it.

She meowed again, glancing over her shoulder to the doorway and then back to Georgie.

"Right," he said, leaving the tome where he'd found it. "I'll just be leaving, then."

Chapter Seventeen

It has long been theorized that the study of the Necromantic Arts would be greatly improved if one could manage the effect's of time. While a person has their own expiration date, their body has another. Science has shown us we can delay this, but eventually, dust returns to dust. This is the reason you will never find a clock in a Necromancer's home. It's far too irritating a reminder that the world does not wait for us.

\- The Dying Art of Necromancy, *Author Unknown*

* * *

Satisfied that he'd done all he could, Georgie returned home.

Yawning, he tumbled through the front door. His father was in early from the forge, rustling about the house and… whistling? The dust cloth in his father's hands looked comically small, and his forge's apron was spattered with dust bunnies instead of ash. The various shelves that had long lain stuffed with various trinkets, always carefully dusted but never disturbed, now lay bare.

Georgie peered into the crates on the table. "What are you doing?"

The Blacksmith halted mid-tune. "Tidying."

Seeing Georgie's curious look, he explained. "Elisa—Your aunt needed Ellory at home, so I finished at the forge early today. I'd thought I'd…" He trailed away as Georgie stepped closer.

Georgie reached inside the crate, gently removing a small vase with dried flowers. "Wasn't this Mum's?"

The Blacksmith's face fell for a moment. With a deep sigh, he sat down at the table. "Sit with me, Georgie."

Georgie did so. His father's beard twitched as he chewed the inside of his cheek. "I, uh…I suppose I wanted to ask your permission," he said slowly. "I…" He ran his hand through his hair. "Giant's teeth." A rare curse fell from his lips. "This is difficult."

Georgie's heart sped up in his chest with an all-too-familiar fear. "Whatever you need to tell me," Georgie said as softly as he could, as if he could soften the blow that had him already crumbling, "it's all right."

The Blacksmith let out a nervous breathy laugh. "Right. Of course. Your aunt…Elisa…she… Well, I hope she will spend more time with us soon. I've asked her to. This house is large enough for us, I think, and it will be good to have her around more."

"Do you need more help?" Georgie asked. "I can—"

The Blacksmith raised his hand. "No, you've done more than enough, son. Truly. Elisa is willing and is probably having a similar discussion with Ellory. But this…this will change things, Georgie. And I wanted to know if it would be all right if…if I moved some of your mother's things."

"What?"

"Nothing will be thrown out," he rushed to say. "Whatever

you want to keep, we can find a place for it. Perhaps we can rotate out some of the books from your room or simply put these away until we need them again."

This was worse than it had ever been. The Blacksmith had always been so careful with Georgie's mum's things, reverent even. What could possibly have happened to make him want to put it all away? But his father was looking at him so expectantly and with so much uncertainty that Georgie knew he couldn't push the matter.

"It's all right, Da," said Georgie. "Whatever you need."

The Blacksmith ducked his head to meet Georgie's lowered eyes. "Are you certain?"

Georgie nodded, his throat too tight to speak.

"It'll be for the best, son," said the Blacksmith, reaching out his large hand to cover Georgie's. "I promise."

But as his father went back to cleaning, Georgie's anxiety whirled about his head in spiraling thoughts, a mixture of images, smells, and words as he tried to sort it all out.

Georgie's guilt at being away from his father gnawed at him. He should have been here. Clearly, the more time he spent away from his da, the worse he was getting.

But the Necromancer also needed his help.

It felt like the one thing he could do. If his magic was helpful or even his intuition, to keep the Necromancer in good shape so that he could keep the Creature away? That was important.

Georgie could only hope that Aunt Elisa could keep an eye on the Blacksmith. She was a stubborn sort. Surely she would know and would tell Georgie if he was needed back home.

One step at a time, he told himself. But the ticking clock on the bare mantel mocked him as the twitching hands pointed towards the photograph of his mother.

* * *

Georgie's dread followed him into the next day. He wrestled with wanting to stay behind to talk to Aunt Elisa, but in the end, seeing the bare shelves and finding his father already at the forge proved too much. He made the trek up the hill to the Necromancer's cottage in forlorn silence, his footsteps echoing the ticking clock in his head.

"You're distracted," the Necromancer observed. Georgie had been staring at the same volunteer skull for twenty minutes with little success.

"Sorry," he mumbled, rubbing at his temples. His own head was pulsing in pain every few seconds.

No time. No time. No time.

"Breathe," said the Necromancer. "And try again. Remember your intentions."

Georgie furrowed his brow, glaring down at the skull on the table in front of him. He had to do this. If he couldn't, then what hope did he have? His father couldn't wait forever. But neither could he.

There was a faint breeze, brushing Georgie's hair against his cheek, but it wasn't enough. Not yet.

The Void gave a low meow of warning.

"Hush, Void," murmured the Necromancer, keeping his eyes trained on his apprentice, even when the moths on the walls began to flutter.

Georgie continued to reach out towards the skull, imagining his open palm, ready to grasp whatever he could. He needed his mother. If his da was putting things away, it had to mean that he was close to giving up. If he hadn't already. Georgie didn't know what that would mean for him, but surely, Adelaide was the only one who could fix this. After all, it was her death that had caused all the trouble in the first place. Georgie was doing all that he could, but it wasn't enough. He couldn't carry all of this alone.

"Focus, Georgie," said the Necromancer as the moths began beating their wings faster and faster on the walls.

But all Georgie could see was the ever-silent skull, his own failure, and his still-empty palm.

With a shout of anger, Georgie knocked the skull away. The skull fell onto the floor with a dull thud, rolling away as dead as it had ever been. The Necromancer stood up just as quickly, his hand outstretched towards him.

"I can't do it," said Georgie, dropping his head into his folded arms, desperate to hide his frustrated tears from his mentor. "I can't bring back anything to life. Not even a stupid skull!"

The Necromancer's voice was unusually subdued. "What do you mean, you can't?"

The angry retort died on Georgie's lips as a cold breath of undead air whooshed across his hair from behind. Slowly, he raised his head to look.

The stuffed bear decorating the cottage was alive.

No, not alive. Animated. It stood on its hind legs, steady as if it were still on its pedestal behind him. The friendly wave was gone, but the claws were still sharp and within arm's reach of Georgie. The bear's chest cracked and groaned against its stuffing as it took in another deep breath.

"Don't make any sudden movements," warned the Necromancer.

That wouldn't be a problem, as Georgie sat, too stunned to move.

The bear's glass eyes did not blink, but they shone with a keen spark of blue light. Had that come from him? But there was something else now.

"Do you feel it? The tether?" asked the Necromancer. "Your emotions are bound to this creature. What are you feeling?"

"Scared," said Georgie. "It's scared." Both undead and caster watched each other warily, waiting for the other to move.

"Is that all?"

The tether between caster and undead reverberated like a plucked harp string. It was a strange sensation. Georgie was familiar with reaching out to determine how others felt around him. Whether it was through careful perception or judging the mood in the air, he had gotten good at it. But for the first time in a long time, Georgie was looking at himself.

He was scared of failing, of being left alone once his father disappeared entirely beneath his grief. The bear took a step back before falling forward onto all fours. Georgie was tired. So tired. Tired from lack of sleep, but more than that, Georgie was tired from trying over and over to prevent something that seemed determined to happen.

With a slight grunt, the bear butted its head into Georgie's chest and stayed there.

Suddenly, the terror faded into that long-buried need for comfort. Georgie wrapped his arms around the bear's head and began quietly crying into its fur.

He'd done it. He'd actually performed Necromancy. He hadn't failed. Not yet.

The Necromancer spoke again. "The day you came to me demanding that I teach you, I gave you a test. I gathered your tears and tested your intentions with flame. The reason you are still here today is because of what spilled out from your heart," he said softly. "Love, sacrifice, and not a single thought for yourself. Your tears were for others who suffered. It is a rare and beautiful thing."

It felt strange to be known and seen. Georgie wanted to squirm away from the brightness of it and also stay in its warm light a little longer.

The bear's steady breaths slowly began to fade as Georgie regained his composure. The tether was drifting away.

"Georgie, it's time to let it go," said the Necromancer.

The bear snorted, burrowing deep into Georgie's chest for one final moment. With a deep breath of his own, Georgie released it. There was another flash of blue light and a rush of cold air as the Necromancer took control. The bear grew stiff once more, its marble eyes dull again as it shambled back towards its pedestal at the Necromancer's command.

Georgie wiped at his cheeks, aware of the Necromancer's keen attention upon him. "What were you thinking of just then?" he asked, his voice still uncharacteristically gentle.

"My mother," Georgie admitted.

The Necromancer nodded to himself. "You were close, then?"

Georgie shook his head, releasing a sigh as well as his confession. "No. Not at all." He hung his head. "Most days, I barely remember her. But I feel like I should. Everyone around me misses her so much, and it feels like I barely knew her. I *want* to miss her. I *should* miss her. But I…I don't. Is that wrong?"

The Necromancer tapped his chin thoughtfully. "Grief is a funny thing. Sometimes we grieve what we never knew."

"It doesn't feel like grief."

"Yes, it may look quite different from what those around you are experiencing. But it is still grief and still important."

"I don't want to grieve," said Georgie. "I don't want to get lost in it like my…"

The Necromancer's eyebrows rose expectantly.

"Like my da," he finished, and finally, the floodgates were opened. "She shouldn't have died! I know it was an accident, but it shouldn't have happened. She should be here with him, to help him. If she were, maybe he wouldn't be the way that he is. Everyone would be happier."

"But she isn't," said the Necromancer.

"But that's just it," said Georgie. "She should be!"

"Why? You seem to do well enough on your own. Wouldn't she get in the way?"

"No!" Georgie's voice rose. "I need her to help me!"

As soon as the words had left his mouth, Georgie felt the last piece of a puzzle slip into place. The truth of it all stunned him into silence.

The Necromancer nodded to himself. "I thought as much. Your earlier chattering the other day was a sure sign of it. The flames showed no thought for yourself, but that isn't always a good thing. Especially when we are hiding truths from ourselves."

Georgie felt embarrassed by his own admission. It felt selfish when he knew he could shoulder the weight of his mother's loss far better than everyone else around him. Was it wrong to miss a person when all you needed was their help? He didn't know the answer yet. But he did finally understand what he'd long buried away.

"Yes. Yes, I miss her," said Georgie.

"You still intend to bring her back, then, don't you?"

"Have you never wanted to bring anyone back?" Georgie asked. There was a moment of silence as Georgie's mission hung in the air between them. He waited for the Necromancer to scold him, to catch it and crush it.

The Necromancer's gaze flickered with magic. "If I have my way, no one will ever need to." He leaned on the table across from Georgie, folding his hands in front of him. "There are lots of 'should's in this world, Georgie. Great injustice, tragedy, and unfairness. We all say it 'shouldn't have happened,' and we're right. None of these things are meant to be. The problem with 'should' is that it doesn't leave room for action. We get caught up in the 'what should have been' versus the way things are. We can shout at the void—beg your pardon, cat—all the 'should's in the world." He reached out with his slender hand, poking Georgie directly in the chest above his heart. "But it is up to us to take what we have and make it better."

"How do I do that, though?"

"Well, for starters…" The Necromancer grinned as he stood. "You could have simply talked with that skull. Instead, you put enough emotional resonance into a bear that your outburst was negated with careful intent, thus making it as gentle as your heart is."

"Why didn't it stay angry?" asked Georgie. "I was angry before."

The Necromancer thought about this for a moment. "Perhaps it is because your anger, while reasonable, was merely a side effect of your inner turmoil. Anger is a quick emotion. It flares as quickly as a flame, but unless there is enough fuel for it, it burns away. Necromancy has a way of getting to the heart of the matter. There are other, stronger emotions that most Necromancers never allow themselves to explore in favor of this quick burst of power. I don't think that will be the case for you. Well done."

Georgie flushed from the praise. "Thank you, sir. For everything."

"My dear boy, we're just getting started."

Chapter Eighteen

Despite the certainty of this decision, there are those who would sway a Necromancer from their chosen quest. Whether it is by starting rumors, taking away funds, or worse still, spreading seeds of doubt, you must hold fast. Doubt to a Necromancer is as dangerous as a hairline fracture. Such things are painful, persistent, and unable to hold any weight without shattering. Thus, I cling to my own mission with the grip of the dead. No one will dissuade me from this. No one. Not even her.

  - The Dying Art of Necromancy, *Author Unknown*

* * *

Over the next few days, Georgie made remarkable progress. Now he could cause the entire collection of animated death's-head moths to fly about the room and then back to their proper pins. He didn't fully animate the bear again, though he could have sworn he saw it wink at him when he successfully held a conversation with a skull that the Necromancer had named 'Ivan'.

But with each and every discovery, there was always more. Georgie rose earlier each morning, eager to run up the hill to practice before his formal teaching began. He barely had time to worry about his father when he was so focused on his books in the evenings. Nor had he seen Aunt Elisa or Ellory yet. But when he did look up, mostly to reach blindly for his empty mug, their presence was felt. He could see his aunt in the freshly baked bread on the counter in the evenings and found Ellory in the ink stains on the table, poorly hidden beneath the embroidered place mats.

Even as Georgie snuck out before dawn, Yoricsgrave was also bustling with excitement. Today was the celebration of the Strands. The leaves on the trees were turning their customary gold, while long wooden tables were stretched out to prepare for the feasting. The first of the autumn flowers were gathered up in large armfuls and woven about the fence posts. The celebratory air was infectious, putting an extra bolt of excitement in his steps .

There was a long, slow-moving line of people coming into town. Families from other villages were arriving in big caravans, bringing with them fluffy sheep, eager to win the prize of the most wool. Farmers with oversized vegetables kept close watch on the carts as diligently as a mother with a newborn babe. Georgie spied a gigantic squash, several enormous pumpkins, and a potato that he mistook for a small child. The Village Watchman, an older man with black skin, named Fredrick, carefully eyed each and every cart. It was a familiar enough sight, and Georgie paid it little mind.

Until a very tall woman in purple approached.

"Thank you so very much for your hospitality, Watchman Frederick," said the Enchantress. She had her own pack slung over her shoulder and an elegant walking stick in her right hand. "It has been an honor."

Georgie ducked behind a cart, ignoring the indignant squawk of the farmer's wife as he jostled it. If the Enchantress was indeed leaving Yoricsgrave, the Necromancer would want to know.

"Are you sure you can't stay for the Strands, ma'am?" asked Frederick. "It'll be a sight to behold for sure, and there's plenty of food for all."

"Thank you," she replied. "But there are others who need me now that your hills are safe again."

The farmer's wife from earlier raised a rag towards Georgie, shooing him away like a nosy fly. Georgie muttered an apology, quickly darting across the lane to get closer.

"You're certain it wasn't a wild animal?" the Watchman asked.

"Quite certain," the Enchantress replied. "I've spoken to several woodland villagers, and none have reported any wild animals of such a nature. I highly doubt that such a creature will harm your festivities, or your travelers."

Was the Creature gone then? Georgie would have to ask Ellory if she'd heard of any further incidents. He couldn't recall any. But perhaps it was less that the Creature had wandered off and merely that the Enchantress was taking the trouble away with her.

"You're an awful lot more helpful than that fellow on the hill up there," said Frederick with a laugh. "We went to him first, you know. And do you know what he says to me?" He took a breath and then out of his mouth came an astonishingly comical impression of the Necromancer. "'Have you hunted down and killed this creature yet? Until that happens, I am no use to you. Fetch yourselves a Woodsman,' he says. So I told him, 'If the Old Woodsman were still walking about, I wouldn't be here, sir.' You'll never guess what he said to that!"

"Oh, do tell," said the Enchantress.

"He says, 'Wouldn't that be a trick?'" Frederick threw back his head and laughed. The Enchantress joined him, but even from his hiding spot, Georgie could tell that her smile was strained.

Georgie slowly crept around them, keeping close to the wall to avoid the Enchantress's line of sight. He felt a little bad. She'd been kind to him, and he hadn't the heart to throw away her scarf. But neither was he eager to strike up a conversation. He almost made it out of the gate and up the path when a red squirrel darted down the path towards him, scaling him as quickly as a tree. Georgie yelped in alarm, battering his hands wildly at the squirrel as it leapt off of his back.

The Enchantress caught sight of him immediately. "Good morning, Georgie!"

"Morning," he replied, glaring in the direction of the unrepentant animal. The squirrel climbed up the Enchantress's staff, obviously pleased with itself.

"Headed back up to the cottage for lessons, then?" the Enchantress asked as she fell into stride with him.

"Yes, ma'am."

"How is he?" she asked, her eyes straight ahead at the path in front of him.

"He's fine. Better than fine, actually." Georgie picked up his pace, hoping that she wouldn't follow him all the way up the hill. He needed the Necromancer to be as clearheaded as possible to avoid another setback in his lessons.

"Tristan Ebenezer is a brilliant man," she said. "In our younger years, he was a brilliant student but intense. As was our instructor, Sardis. He was a strict man and unforgiving to his students. I don't know what happened to make him as harsh as he was, but he never relented in the many years that I knew him." Her purple eyes fell on Georgie. "I want to make sure Tristan is not repeating his mentor's mistakes with you."

He felt suddenly very defensive of the Necromancer. "He's not like that. He's a great tutor, and I'm learning a lot. He doesn't talk about Sardis at all."

"That doesn't surprise me. Sardis was always a difficult person."

"The Necromancer said that you stopped studying when it got too difficult," Georgie retorted.

The Enchantress's head snapped towards him. "It would be easier for him to accept if that were true," she replied. "I left because of Sardis. Not because I lack in magical skill. It was unacceptable for any teacher to treat a child that way, brilliant or otherwise. I asked Tristan to go with me, to transfer elsewhere, or simply run away from it all, but he refused. The work was too important to him, and Sardis's claws had dug too deep." The Enchantress gave a dismissive toss of her hair. "Clearly, he hasn't forgiven me yet."

Georgie didn't like the sudden guilt that gnawed at him. He'd been unfair to the Enchantress, and she was right to call him out for it.

"I don't understand," said Georgie. "Why are you telling me all of this if you're leaving?"

The Enchantress sighed. "I want you to be careful, Georgie, especially around the Necromancer. I'm worried that his old wounds might lead him down a path too dark for you to follow." Her eyes drifted towards the hilltop again, as if she could peer directly into the Necromancer's cottage. Georgie wasn't certain of all the nuances of enchantment magic, but perhaps she could.

Georgie thought about the Necromancer's bad days and wondered just how many of those the Enchantress had seen.

Perhaps that was the cause for her concern. "I'll be careful," he said. "But he really is doing better, promise. I'm taking good care of him."

The Enchantress wiped her cheek, brushing aside a lingering tear. "I'm sure you are." She squeezed Georgie's shoulder. He wondered if that'd been for his reassurance or hers.

Thankfully, the Enchantress did not follow Georgie all the way to the Necromancer's house. Instead, she parted ways with him as the path split. Georgie would continue to head up the mountain, while she would go through the pass itself.

"Take care, Georgie," she said. "Think about what I've said, and perhaps we'll meet again someday."

Georgie did his best to leave her concerns on the path behind him. It wouldn't do him good to doubt the Necromancer now. If the Creature was indeed gone, Georgie reasoned that the Necromancer would have more time for teaching, which in turn meant Georgie could learn more.

Had it only been a few weeks since he'd walked this path, desperate for a way forward? Now he had it. His steps were as certain as the familiar road ahead. He would find the way to bring his mother back—and soon.

* * *

"Georgie! You're here!" the Necromancer shouted as he threw open the cottage door. "Come, come quickly! We have much to do today!"

Georgie eagerly ran forward, setting his pack down at the door. The Necromancer's back was turned to him as he quickly threw all manner of tea leaves haphazardly into a dented kettle.

"It is a good day," he said, turning around with a flourish. "The most auspicious and excellent of mornings!"

Georgie stepped back. The Necromancer's eyes, normally cool and blue, were bloodshot, while the circles beneath them were as dark as a grave. His clothes were splattered with mud and smelled less like the herbs he carried and more of a damp mold.

"Did you…sleep all right, sir?" Georgie asked, even with all the evidence to the contrary before him.

"Sleep?" The Necromancer smiled, a wide and rabid grin, as he set down a teacup on the desk. "Sleep is for the dead." He threw back his cup of tea, smacking his lips together with great satisfaction.

Georgie sipped politely at his own cup, suddenly glad the Enchantress had left when she had.

"Herbert will attend to your lecture today," said the Necromancer as he opened the door to the closet. The Void hissed and ran as more clutter fell out onto the floor, while Herbert leaned out of the doorway like an unannounced guest. The Necromancer motioned for Georgie to take a seat at his desk while he wheeled Herbert over in front of it. "I have matters to attend to in the tower this morning," he said. "But I won't be far." He started to chant before pausing, smiling over his shoulder at Georgie. "Would you care to do the honors?"

It took a few tries as Georgie rolled the unfamiliar words around his mouth like a new food, but within minutes, the icy breeze of Necromancy blew through the cottage as Herbert's skeletal frame shook to life. The skeleton's mouth hung open, the strange, chilled breath lingering where his lungs would have hung.

"The Notable Figures of Necromancy, if you'd be so kind,"

instructed the Necromancer.

The skeleton stared at him with empty eye sockets. A small black silk ribbon lay tied about the top of his spine where the squirrel had dislodged his skull. The injury added an extra layer of horror as the skeleton gave an undead semblance of a nod.

"Study hard," said the Necromancer as he headed out the door. "Scream into the Void if you need me for anything!" The cat in question hopped up on the desk, sitting next to Georgie's ink and quill with as much disdain as an ancient animal could muster.

"The Notable Figures of Necromancy from the last five centuries," began Herbert. "Recited in reverse chronological order starting in the year 237 P.V.

"Figure five hundred and thirteen," continued Herbert. "Harlequin Bandino."

The next two hours passed by slowly. Georgie dutifully took notes as Herbert described the various historical figures who'd dabbled in Necromancy. But after a while, even the speaking dead grew boring. Georgie's concentration faded, causing Herbert's perky lecture to slow to a mind-numbing hum. Georgie felt his eyes drooping. The Void had already shamelessly fallen asleep on the desk, dead to the world.

"Figure one. Kaspar Cynward."

Georgie nearly fell out of his chair. "What?"

The Void, startled by this, leapt up with a vicious yowl and scampered off the desk, scattering Georgie's notes to the floor. He didn't have time to gather them as Herbert was still talking, his bony jaw moving up and down like a marionette.

"The earliest recorded master of the Necromantic Arts. Born in 543 G.D., he is responsible for the development, study, and integration of Necromancy into the College of Magi. At the behest of King Sylas the Besieged, he singlehandedly put an end to the Giant Uprising. He fell in this pursuit with a recorded time of death of 0 P.V. Due to this victory, the calendar year was changed in his honor, with the years following recorded as 'Post Victory.' He was posthumously titled by King Sylas as 'The Death-Weaver.'"

Georgie's heart raced in his chest. Memories of that night in the Crypt flashed before his eyes. The carvings inside the mausoleum that he'd thought had been sunbeams hadn't been that at all. They'd been threads. The Death-Weaver was here, buried in Yoricsgrave, of all places.

"Whilst his historical significance is without question, the nature of his research is a carefully guarded secret. It was said that his life's work dabbled in the arcane pursuit of resurrection. If this was the case, it has been lost to time. There are no further records regarding him." The skeleton sighed, crumbling inward as the magic left him.

"No, no, no. Wait!" Georgie said, running up to Herbert. "Why was it lost? Why is he buried here?"

But Herbert stood slumped forward on his stand, dead silent.

Georgie grabbed at his hair and paced. The ballad that Herbert had told him the first day about the Death-Weaver surely had more information. The Necromancer had told him it was up to him to discover what it meant. He was close to something. So close. But the pieces of it all seemed to fly through his fingers like wisps of smoke.

He would have to animate Herbert again. Perhaps he could get him to speak the ballad once more. The spell was on the tip of his tongue before the Necromancer stepped through the door.

"You look like you've seen a ghost," he said.

Georgie was at a loss for words. He couldn't openly ask the Necromancer about Kaspar. It would only reveal that he had been in the locked mausoleum and snooping after him in the dead of night with Ellory.

The answer lay before him as bright as his cousin's mischievous grin. Of course! Ellory! If she could get him into the crypt again, Georgie could speak to Kaspar himself. He could ask him for the secret of resurrection. Georgie could bring back his mother.

He had to talk to Ellory as soon as possible.

The Necromancer didn't seem to notice Georgie's distress. He chuckled to himself. "Though I suppose Herbert could count as a ghost. But at least he's friendly. There was a time when I met another called—"

"Let's go into town!" Georgie blurted out.

The Necromancer blinked owlishly. "Go into town?"

Georgie nodded quickly, gathering up the papers on the floor in a semblance of cleaning up. "It's not far. Probably even easier to get there at first because it's all downhill. Surely you've gone there before."

"I know where the town is." The Necromancer straightened up. "I simply see no need to go there."

"But there's a festival today," said Georgie, tossing the papers down on the desk. "The Strands! Everyone will be there, and you shouldn't miss it."

The wizard hesitated, his eyes darting back and forth between Georgie and the tower. The Void stepped between them, rubbing herself against the Necromancer's legs.

"I suppose I have earned a bit of celebration, haven't I?" said the Necromancer, speaking mostly to the cat in front of him, then to Georgie. The Void gave forth a disjointed roll of thunder as she purred in agreement. The Necromancer gave a reluctant sigh and a nod. "Right, then. Let me gather my things."

Chapter Nineteen

It is a peculiar quirk of humanity that sees the past as forever further away than it actually is. Time does strange things to the past. It either brightens it, scraping away all rough edges into a small speck of untouchable bliss, or disposes of itself entirely. Even so, there are specks to be found. Whether it is a phrase, a curse, a traditional handcraft, or even a road that is used because 'it always has been,' the past has a way of lingering, just beneath the surface. Even my own past is a stain far too stubborn to scrub out.

\- The Dying Art of Necromancy, *Author Unknown*

***

In but a few moments, Georgie was leading the Necromancer down the hillside. It was as if his own shadow had grown larger, the lithe, tall frame of the Necromancer, still in his black cloak despite the bright sun, stretching out behind him. The Void trotted at their heels, tail upright and twitching with distrust at every falling leaf that passed.

Georgie was lost in his own thoughts. Kaspar Cynward, the Death-Weaver, was buried in Yoricsgrave! But more than that was the promise of Kaspar's studies in resurrection, true resurrection. Had that been what the Necromancer had wanted him to discover? That the secret he sought was actually buried here? And if that were the case, why was the Necromancer still so insistent that true resurrection couldn't be done when the very key lay hidden in the valley?

He barely noticed when the Necromancer stopped at the edge of town until the Void yowled at him.

"What's wrong?" Georgie asked, trotting back up the hill towards the Necromancer.

"Nothing," he replied, adjusting the pin to his cloak. "Simply preparing."

Georgie suddenly realized that the Necromancer wasn't used to people. He supposed it would be quite a unique experience to go from dictating the conversation with the dead to suddenly being thrown amongst the living.

He gave his mentor a reassuring smile. "It'll be all right. Come on!"

The village square was as lively as it had ever been, and the cobblestones hummed underneath their feet from the crowd. There were brightly painted carts on every street corner as every villager was out selling their wares. There was Mr. Vessar, proudly filling up his customers' baskets with enormous summer produce. Mrs. Accola and her wife were walking about, arm in arm, while holding tightly to the leashes of their four eager dogs. Bubbles floated in the air from the toymaker's stall, barely seen over the crowd of jostling children in front of it. The giant vegetable contest was ongoing as the group of judges wandered about the various carts with clipboards and measuring tapes in hand.

Georgie kept close to the Necromancer's side, gently tugging his sleeve so he wouldn't be in the way of the stilt performers who walked around town. Some stood at eight feet tall, while others reached heights of twelve feet. Even smaller children, learning how to use them for the first time, toddled about on the stilts barely a foot high.

The Necromancer eyed them with a furrowed brow as they waved at him. "They look like giants. Is this normal?"

Georgie had never considered it. "It happens every year, as far as I know."

"Attention, friends!" boomed Watchman Frederick from the center of the square. "The naming of the Spinner Sisters is about to begin!"

"They pick three women of the village to oversee the Dance of the Strands," explained Georgie. "That's what the pole is for."

The Necromancer gave a frown. "I see."

Perhaps it had been unwise to convince the Necromancer to attend, especially considering that he hadn't slept the night before. He certainly didn't seem to be enjoying himself at all. But it was too late now, and Georgie still needed to find Ellory. If she was anywhere, it was in the crowd. She wouldn't miss the Strands for all the world.

"And finally, our youngest Spinner, Miss Ellory Harper!"

His cousin bounded up the steps to the stage, beaming brightly as her ceremonial flower crown was placed upon her head. She reverently accepted the pair of shears from the Priest, snapping them a few times with a dangerous curiosity. The oldest of the Sisters placed her hand gently over top of hers, indicating she should stop. Georgie was proud of his cousin. She was clearly enjoying the attention, but it would be much harder to approach her now.

"Let the dance of the Strands begin!"

There was a loud cheer as the stilted performers stepped

forward. They grabbed the highest bound silks, while each of the Sisters, Ellory included, grabbed their own ends. The musicians began to play with thundering drums, a stern march, while bright flutes played the melody overtop.

It's a Sister's work to mind the strands
The three of them are glad to mend
Life and love and joy and pain
They mind them all again, again,

But then one day, there came a man
Who thought he knew much better than them
Life and love and joy and pain
He tied his knots again, again,

He wrapped them to his wrists and feet
The Strands were bound with his heart beat
Life and love and joy and pain
He risked his life again, again

Now listen close to those who hear
Man is never to interfere
Life and love and joy and pain
The Sisters caught him again, again,

The knots held fast, the Strands lay tied
The foolish man tore up and died
Life and love and joy and pain
They mourned for him again, again

So now we remember in dance and song

That fateful day when man was wrong
Life and love and joy and pain
The Strands hold fast again, again

The villagers, stilted and small, danced as they sang. Some held on to their golden threads with both hands, while others used tambourines against their thighs as they marched. They danced and danced, repeating the song twice over as their threads wound up the pole, higher and higher. The Strands left the wooden pole, crawling up the cornstalk effigy at the top. The oversized head wobbled back and forth until finally, it popped.

A loud cheer went out over the crowd as the dancers below were covered in red flower petals and small wrapped treats that the children scrambled to pick up. Further announcements were made from the stage as the ceremonial Sisters were ushered away.

Georgie stood on his tiptoes, trying to catch sight of Ellory before she disappeared into the crowd. "Come on. We have to—"

The Necromancer was gone.

"Sir?" Georgie called. "Sir?"

He found the Necromancer in a dark alleyway, leaning back against the shadowed stone. At some point in their walk, the Necromancer had picked up the Void. Georgie was shocked that she'd allowed anyone to touch her, much less carry her, but the cat perched around the Necromancer's shoulders like an inky-black collar.

"*Mata ruumiita,*" swore the Necromancer. "What is this festival?"

"It's the Strands," said Georgie, approaching him with open palms. The Necromancer's face was shining with sweat. The

Void gave a low meow under the duress of the Necromancer's frantic strokes. "You don't like crowds, do you?" asked Georgie.

"Not my favorite," the Necromancer replied, his voice cracking even as he tried to joke.

"Wait here," said Georgie. "I'll fetch you some water."

It didn't take long to find a vendor nor grab a cup of fresh dandelion tea with ice. But as he was running back to the Necromancer, he tripped.

The drink spilled out onto the cobblestone s as Fitz's boot kicked the remaining puddle into Georgie's face. "Tripped on your own feet, did you?"

"Not now, Fitz," growled Georgie. "Leave me alone."

"Stay." The bully pushed him back down into the dirt. "I've been wanting to talk. Heard you've been taking lessons with the freak on the hilltop."

"Shut. Up. Fitz," said Georgie, clenching his fists.

But Fitz wasn't smart enough to listen. "Come on, then, Georgie. Let's see your magic tricks!"

A tall shadow fell over them both. "Tada."

The Necromancer loomed out of the darkness, his pale-white hand gripping on to Fitz's shoulder. "That wasn't very kind."

The Void hissed from her perch on the Necromancer's shoulders in agreement.

Fitz shoved the Necromancer's hand off of him. "What are you going to do about it?"

A slow, skull-like grin crept across the Necromancer's face. "Oh, I can do a great many things."

Fitz backed up as the Necromancer approached, a threat in each step. "I will melt your bones into ash where you stand. I can make your teeth dance in your skull. But more importantly…" The Necromancer leaned in very close, his breath suddenly cold with frost. "I can make your bones carry your body away as easily as a puppet on a string."

There was a flash of blue lightning from the Necromancer's eyes, and Fitz ran away screaming.

The Necromancer straightened, wiping his hand distastefully on his cloak. "I despise bullies."

"T-Thank you?" said Georgie, getting off the ground. "Sorry that I dropped the water, sir."

"Not a problem. I'm feeling quite refreshed now," the Necromancer said. "He shouldn't trouble you again. At least not if he knows what is good for him."

Georgie gulped. "Could you really do all that?"

The Necromancer didn't look at him. "I don't hurt children, Georgie." A pause. "But probably."

"Georgie! There you are! I've been looking all over for you!" Ellory came bounding up to them. She gave a shy wave to the Necromancer. "Oh, hello again."

The Necromancer gave a stiff nod back.

Ellory grabbed a hold of Georgie's arm. "We have so much to discuss."

"We really do," he agreed. "This morning, I—" He paused. "Wait, what are you talking about?"

Ellory's jaw dropped. "You're kidding, right? I'd have thought you'd have figured it out by now."

Had his cousin really discovered the secret of the Death-Weaver without him? It was possible. She was incredibly smart. But he couldn't help but feel a bit crushed. "You knew?"

She rolled her eyes at him, looping her arm in his. "Come on. We'll talk back at the house."

The Necromancer was still there, trying dutifully to ignore the conversation he wasn't a part of.

Georgie looked at Ellory and then back at the Necromancer. "Would you like to meet my da?"

The Necromancer couldn't hide his grimace fast enough. "Georgie, I really best be off. It's almost time that I—"

"It's on the edge of town," added Ellory helpfully.

"It's true," said Georgie. "And I want to check on him before we go back. If that's all right with you."

"Is he ill?" asked the Necromancer.

"No, but he forgets to look after himself sometimes."

The Necromancer nodded to himself, accepting this without issue.

As they left the village square behind, the Necromancer seemed to relax. His nervous, almost-frantic petting of the Void slowed, much to the creature's comfort.

"I can't believe you didn't know," said Ellory, shaking her head.

"Well, I only just found out about it today," Georgie replied defensively. "It's hard enough just getting him to talk, let alone get information out of him."

"That's true. Your da is very secretive."

Georgie stopped in the middle of the path. "My da?"

Ellory raised a single eyebrow. "Yes. Who were you talking about?"

By now, they had reached home, and the familiar ring of the forge was strangely silent. Georgie quickened his steps then started jogging, leaving both Ellory and the Necromancer behind as the silence stretched on.

Had his father fallen ill? Was he even at the forge?

He skidded to a halt at the doorway; the warmth emanated from inside as the forge lay lit. His father sat at his workbench, a plate of food in front of him.

"Ah, Georgie!" he called out, waving the boy over. "You're home early."

Georgie blinked in confusion. "You're…eating?"

The Blacksmith gave a crooked smile. "It's noon, isn't it? Have you eaten yourself?"

"Not yet, but…" Georgie trailed off as the Necromancer's shadow stretched behind him. "I wanted you to meet someone."

The Necromancer looked about the forge, sniffing as if to discover what chemicals were being used. His blue eyes darted about, carefully taking in each tool and instrument with precision.

"Alistair Smith," said the Blacksmith, holding out his hand.

The Necromancer shook the offered hand in his own once, dropping it quickly. "Charmed."

The Blacksmith raised a curious brow but pressed on. "I'm grateful for your offer to teach my son. His mother was magically inclined, so it is good to know that he'll be able to carry that part of her forward."

The Necromancer's face grew impossibly pale. "Right. Yes. Of course. The mother."

"Is he all right?" Ellory whispered into Georgie's ear. But all Georgie could do was watch in horror as the Necromancer kept speaking.

"It's quite a large undertaking, but your son, like your wife, appears to be very dead…dedicated! Yes. That's the word. Dedicated."

Georgie wanted to crawl beneath the dirt with secondhand embarrassment.

"So, um…congratulations are in order, I think…" The Necromancer finally trailed off. "To your son. And your bride."

The Blacksmith tilted his head. "My bride? Who told you?"

The Necromancer stammered again when Aunt Elisa stepped in from behind them all. "Alistair! You didn't tell me we had company!" She wrapped her arms around the Blacksmith's shoulders, placing a kiss on his cheek.

The sudden show of affection startled Georgie. His aunt had never behaved in such a way. But as he stared at them, his eyes fell to the simple, glimmering gold band on Aunt Elisa's left hand.

"Georgie's tutor was just offering us congratulations," the Blacksmith explained. "Have you told everyone all ready?"

Aunt Elisa admired the ring on her finger with a soft smile. "Not yet, but I couldn't help wearing it out."

Georgie nearly lost his footing again, tripping over the truth that lay before him with astonishing clarity.

His father and Aunt Elisa were engaged.

Chapter Twenty

I'm close. I can feel it. My goal is within reach. No more setbacks, no more distractions. Time is finally on my side.
  - The Dying Art of Necromancy, *Author Unknown*

* * *

"I can't believe you didn't know!" Ellory exclaimed much later that evening. The Necromancer had quickly excused himself after the brief introduction, returning up the hill towards his cottage with the Void following on his heels.

Georgie sat at the table, still stunned hours later.

His father was going to marry Aunt Elisa.

"It just seems so…sudden?" he said.

Ellory stared at him. "You honestly haven't noticed? They've been in love for years!"

In love? His father?

"From the way Mum tells it," explained Ellory, "he's been working longer hours at the forge to save up to purchase the ring. He bought it the same day he bought my notebook."

The last few weeks took on a startling new light. His father's intense focus, the rearranging of the house—even his awkward talk about change. It made sense for Aunt Elisa and Ellory to live with them. Aunt Elisa wouldn't have to walk from the other side of town every morning, and it would be fun to have Ellory around. But *married*?

The idea didn't bother Georgie. In fact, he was surprised to find that he rather liked it. The house always felt brighter with both Aunt Elisa and Ellory here.

His father's nervousness from the past few days faded before his eyes as they prepared for dinner. His father came in before sunset, closing the forge at a reasonable hour in order to help Aunt Elisa in the kitchen.

The Blacksmith and Aunt Elisa moved around each other in a way that reminded Georgie of dancing. There was a warm familiarity between them, now that his father's nervousness had faded away. It was there in the small, lingering glances that Aunt Elisa gave his father, and in the way the Blacksmith's hands gently touched her waist as he stepped past.

It was strange to see his father as a romantic. But of course he was. How could he not be after the death of his first wife had left him so broken? Georgie wondered what it had been like with Adelaide. The gentleness and the long looks across the room no longer hidden but cherished.

Ellory caught Georgie looking at them and grinned. "He wasn't sure if she would say 'yes,'" Ellory informed him. "Which is silly because she's been nervous about him never asking."

"I'd half a mind to berate you, showing up on my doorstep at night to demand that I marry you," Aunt Elisa said, giggling like a schoolgirl. She held up her hand to the light to allow the gold to sparkle. "But I can't stop staring at it. It's perfect."

The Blacksmith kissed her cheek, causing Aunt Elisa to giggle once more.

Ellory rolled her eyes but couldn't hide her own smile.

Dinner that night was a lively one. There was a new energy, as if whatever had been tucked away could now breathe. It was warm, loving, and seemed to light up the whole house with a gentle glow.

Aunt Elisa chattered excitedly about the preparations that would need to be made. Ellory eagerly asked after which room would be hers and whether or not she could paint it bright green. Georgie had little to offer in the way of conversation but beamed as the Blacksmith's smile grew wider and wider. Georgie couldn't remember the last time everyone had been so happy. He wished his mother could be here to see it.

The warmth in Georgie's chest turned to an ice-sharp cold. He looked at the mantel for his mother's portrait. The memory of Adelaide lay still on the mantel, but as the sunlight faded, a shadow fell across it. Not forgotten—Georgie could never. But distant. Had the portrait faded that much over time?

The forgetfulness frightened Georgie. How could he get so lost in this happiness to forget what had been lost? She was still gone, and despite the surrounding happiness, the dull pain still echoed in his own heart.

All the stories he'd been told about his mother, what she'd been capable of, and her importance to everything that surrounded him flooded his senses at once. It hurt to think that after all this time of trying to push away the Blacksmith's grief, the answer had lain in someone else. Georgie hadn't been enough. Would Aunt Elisa be?

He loved his aunt, truly, but his doubts lingered. What would Aunt Elisa do if all of her efforts failed? His father's moods were unpredictable. Everything was fine now, but would it stay that way? Or would his father's grief threaten to drown Aunt Elisa and Ellory as well? He didn't want that for her, or Ellory. He didn't want that for himself.

The last few days had brought him closer to his mother than he had ever been before. Working with magic, knowing that someday he might get to hear her voice again, mattered to Georgie more than ever now. There was only one way to fix this, a way that lay back up the hill to the Necromancer's cottage.

"The stronger the emotional bond, the easier it is to summon. If the bond is no longer there, nothing will bring them back."

He was out of time.

* * *

The next morning, Georgie ran to the Necromancer's cottage.

Everything was moving so quickly! His father hadn't seemed bothered with the details of planning a wedding. He might have gone without a large ceremony if he had his way. But Aunt Elisa and Ellory were excited about the possibility of a proper wedding, and the Blacksmith couldn't begrudge them the desire to celebrate. Georgie had a few weeks at best.

It wasn't out of the realm of possibility that the Necromancer knew how to raise the dead. Every single time he arrived at the Necromancer's house, Georgie was constantly surprised at the difference between what he was told and what was actually true.

There had to be some way to bring his mother back.

The Necromancer greeted him. "Morning, Georgie." He sat at the table, the commissioned chain work in front of him. To his right lay a variety of black obsidian glass tools that Georgie had never seen before. The Necromancer took notes with his left hand, the quill scratching across the page with meticulous intent.

Georgie was out of breath by the time he'd arrived, bursting through the door with the last of his speed. "How do you bring someone back from the dead?"

The quill jolted in the Necromancer's hand. With a small, irritated grumble, the Necromancer set the quill down. "You don't."

"But you *could*," said Georgie. "If you wanted to."

The Necromancer's hand brushed the chains on the table. "No."

Georgie went to the other side of the table, leaning against it to meet his tutor's face. "But there are stories of it! You've told me all of them! What about the giants that the Death-Weaver brought back? Or the war lord who requested his brother? Surely there has to be—"

"They're myths, Georgie," the Necromancer insisted. "Tales that serve as a warning to deter anyone from wasting their intellect on an impossible pursuit."

"But what if they're real? What if the truth is in the words of the riddle and the myths all along? You don't know whether or not they *are* truly fake."

The Necromancer's eyes flashed with irritation. "I do. It is written in every text, carved into every skull, and as useless a pursuit as this conversation." He stood, gathering up the chains in his hands to put them away.

"But what about the bird?" asked Georgie.

"The bird is probably dead again by now," said the Necromancer. "If we're lucky, it went in its sleep. A happier end than what it originally met, but an end. Animals are different. Their souls are simpler to animate. You had success with the stuffed bear, yes, but Necromantic magic cannot hold for long, Georgie.

You're placing energy into an already broken vessel. It leaks faster depending on how broken the body is, but eventually, it fades. You'd have to keep pouring more magic into it and replicate your emotions the same each and every time. It's exhausting. Wizards fade away, pouring their lives into empty broken things, into shells."

Georgie clenched his fists at his sides. "You said you'd help me."

"Do you honestly think that those who are gifted in Necromancy are allowed everything that they want?" the Necromancer snapped. "Come now, Georgie, you're smarter than that. If every Necromancer got what they wanted, there would be no end to chaos."

"What was the point of it all, then?" Georgie shouted, slamming his hands down on the table.

The chains in the Necromancer's hands crackled with blue energy. The Void gave a low meow of warning.

"Fine," said the Necromancer, leaving the chains on the table. "I'll show you."

The Necromancer went over to the desk, grabbing the black leather grimoire off of it. He flipped through the pages, his jaw clenched. "Here," he said, throwing the book in front of Georgie.

Even with his own anger still hot in his chest, Georgie gasped. The pages were covered in illustrations. There were diagrams of various dissections, and bloody fingerprints marred the edges of the page. But the most horrifying was a portrait. It was a decomposed body, the muscular structure sloughing off of its frame as it stood, bound up in rope. Its head lay cocked to the side at an unnatural angle while mismatched eyes, plucked from who knew where, stared at the illustrator. They were in agony. The jaw was open in a mournful wail, and whoever had sketched this had been honest enough to include the Creature's tears.

"Why is it bound?" asked Georgie, still staring in horror.

"They're dangerous," replied the Necromancer. "They have the same memories, but the heart is gone. They take on the traits of their maker, then. Whatever emotional energy and magic have been poured into them. I don't think I need to explain what state a person must be in to get this far." The Necromancer closed the book and returned it to the shelf.

But Georgie still had one last card to play. "What about Kaspar Cynward? Could he help?"

The Necromancer went very still. "Where did you hear that name?"

"Herbert told me," said Georgie. "He said that he was working on resurrection rituals. Did you know that he's buried here? In Yoricsgrave? What if we tried to talk to him? He could help! Surely he'd know something as the first Necromancer."

"Listen to me carefully." The Necromancer's voice was deep with warning. "Forget that name. You are not to speak it again. Ever."

It was all the confirmation that Georgie needed. "So you *do* know that he's here."

"I said to forget it!" The Necromancer's voice cracked like a whip, causing the Void to leap off the counter and hide beneath the couch. "I meant it."

"You won't even try!" Georgie accused back. "What are you afraid of? You've talked to Herbert dozens of times, but you won't bother speaking with the only person who could do this?"

"That's enough, Georgie."

"You call the Enchantress weak for abandoning Necromancy.

For not wanting to do what was necessary. How is this any different?"

"ENOUGH!"

The shutters of the cottage slammed closed, plunging the interior into darkness as each light was snuffed. The Necromancer's shadow loomed larger now, growing in size before Georgie.

"I agreed to teach you because I thought you'd be grateful," said the Necromancer. "And this is how you repay me? With a tantrum? You're a foolish and selfish boy who thinks he's already outgrown his tutor."

Georgie trembled, fear and rage mixing together.

"Your mother is dead. And that's all she ever will be, as long as I have anything to do with it." The Necromancer stumbled as he tried to get farther. The Void stood in his path, hissing up at him.

The darkness receded, and the Necromancer's shoulders slumped with weariness. "You're clearly in emotional distress," he said, pushing him aside as he walked past. "Go home. I can't teach you when you're like this." The Necromancer sat down in his chair, facing away from him.

He didn't turn as Georgie wiped his own eyes. Nor did he notice when Georgie snuck over to the shelves. He didn't see Georgie grab the black leather tome, stuff it underneath his shirt, and leave without a word.

Chapter Twenty-One

I was lucky to find this volume when I did. The fact that it is still intact after hundreds of years of burial would be considered a miracle if I believed in such things. Divination Wizards deal in omens. Necromancers deal with the dead. Today, the dead are kind. It's as if he wanted to be found, and all his secrets with him.
  - The Dying Art of Necromancy, *T.E.*

* * *

Georgie stared down at the book in front of him. *The Dying Art of Necromancy* lay as dark as an ink stain on his bedsheets. The silken ribbon pouring out from inside the pages was like a vein of black blood.

What had he been thinking taking this from the Necromancer's house?

He hadn't, and that was the problem. It had been a rush of anger, a sudden desire to act in defiance that had surprised him as much as it had thrilled him. He wasn't familiar with this taking action, but it felt good to be doing something tangible. Besides, as big a problem as it was, it might also be a solution.

Upon closer inspection, the book was far older than he had

initially realized. There were creases in the leather, as if it had once been tightly bound with twine. The pages were thinning pieces of yellow parchment, while the spine lay cracked with the thin, spiderweb-like binding barely holding it together.

The contents were astounding. It was an encyclopedia of Necromantic spells. Starting from the earliest, rudimentary runes and pushing outward into territory that Georgie could scarcely imagine. Some of the earliest spells had faded with time as even a Necromantic ink was subject to decay. All were signed and dated with the initials *T. E.*

There were newer pieces of paper near here where Georgie spied the familiar script of his tutor trying to restore the text. In fact, the Necromancer had left notes all over this tome. He'd left commentary on the practicality of certain spells. He'd hypothesized the use of others, but more importantly, he'd taken notes.

Ropes are proving ineffective, the notes read. *Even the enchanted knot work can become frayed beneath through the sheer wrath of an undead when called with impatience. Something stronger is needed. Perhaps something made of the material the Creature lacks. Iron and blood. And a steadier hand.*

"Georgie? Are you in there?" Ellory's voice called from outside of his door.

"Just a minute!" he replied, scanning the pages for more.

There are spells here, written for the use of resurrection without the nasty business of rebuilding the body's integrity. But the cost is high and the effects fleeting.

Georgie flipped faster.

There, near the beginning of the tome in faded ink, lay a spell entitled 'An Incantation to Resurrect the Dead.'

He'd found it.

Ellory's persistent knocking at his door grew louder. "Georgie. I'm coming in now."

"Wait!" he replied, unable to keep his frustration out of his voice. He slammed the book shut and stuffed it beneath a pile of dirty laundry as Ellory opened the door.

"What are you doing?" Ellory asked, her eyes narrowing suspiciously.

"Reading," said Georgie, keeping it as close to the truth as he could. He hopped down off of the window seat. "Food is ready, right?"

Ellory looked over his shoulder. "Are you going to bring the laundry down with you?"

"I can get it later."

"No need to make two trips," said Ellory, stepping forward. "I can grab it."

"Ellory, wait! Don't!"

But as his cousin scooped up the load of laundry, the grimoire toppled out, falling open to the grim illustration of the Creature inside.

A horrified silence stretched between them as Ellory's eyes went wide. "I knew it."

Georgie quickly scooped up the book. "You can't tell anyone."

"I'm surprised he let you have something like that."

Georgie hesitated. "He doesn't know."

"You *stole* it?" Her voice rose to a fever pitch.

Georgie clutched the book to his chest. "I-I took it without him knowing, yes. But I need it. I think this can help me."

"To bring you closer to your mum?" she asked, placing her hands on her hips. "Or to bring her back?" Quick Ellory had put all the pieces together. He could read it on her face as plain as day. "Why?"

CHAPTER TWENTY-ONE

"Isn't it obvious?" Georgie asked. "Because I have to."

"You're going to mess everything up," she warned.

Georgie shook his head fiercely. "No, I won't. Not if it goes right. I'm going to talk to the Death-Weaver first. Did you know that he's buried here? The original Necromancer, that's Kaspar Cynward. That's what Herbert's ballad and riddle were all about." He opened the book to the earlier, faded page. "Herbert mentioned Kaspar was working on a resurrection ritual. There are notes in here that suggest the same thing. I don't know if he succeeded, but if I can talk to him, like I talk to Herbert, I can find out how."

Ellory's voice was very soft. "Didn't Kaspar die because he kept resurrecting the dead?"

"Only because he did too many at once," Georgie replied, clinging on to that hope as if it were his own life thread. "I only need to do one. Just my mum."

"But then what, Georgie? You're going to walk around, forever bound to your undead mother for the rest of your life?"

He felt like he already was. Every mention of his likeness to his mother drove it home. Every sad look sent his way, and every insult the village boys made felt imbedded in his skin. If she would make his family happy, if she would make him feel whole again, he would do it. "Yes."

Ellory didn't look convinced. In fact, she looked very much like she was about to cry. "Georgie, you can't."

His patience was wearing thin. "If you could bring back your father, wouldn't you at least try?"

Ellory visibly winced. "That's not fair."

"But you would, wouldn't you?" he pressed. "You'd do anything you could?"

"My mum is happy now, though," whispered Ellory. "She's in

love."

Georgie tried not to think about what sort of wedding present that would be. Your newly undead sister and former bride showing up just as new vows were being spoken. "But she'll have her sister back. Perhaps that will help. After all, she misses her."

Now Ellory was crying. Her cheeks were damp with silent tears as she stared at the book in his hands. He knew she would keep his secret if he asked, but all he could do was offer one last plea in the face of her grief. "Ellory, I have to at least try."

She took a deep breath and then squared her shoulders. "Fine. But I'm coming with you."

* * *

It was decided that Georgie should practice his Necromancy outside.

"We should probably get far away from the village," Ellory suggested. "And the graveyard." They stayed clear of the Necromancer's cottage, leaving the path and going beyond it with the tower to their left.

The foothills were quiet. Georgie could still hear the distant fall of the Blacksmith's hammer echoing from the village below. The gentle scent of the surrounding wildflowers was peaceful. With the bright spring sun overhead, Georgie felt sure that the Necromancer's warning of death was overly cautious.

Georgie pulled the Enchantress's scarf from his neck and spread it out along the ground. He didn't know if she would approve of him doing Necromancy, but he felt safer with the scarf nearby. Perhaps her magic would help, too.

The scarf seemed to grow as it lay on the ground, stretching into a wide tapestry of purple and red. "Wow," Ellory breathed, touching it with the tip of her shoe. The scarf fluttered in the breeze for a moment but lay still. Georgie laid the Necromancer's tome in the center before he and Ellory knelt on either side.

"Do you think this is why the Necromancer is here?" Ellory asked. "To guard the grave of the Death-Weaver?"

Georgie remembered the stormy look on the Necromancer's face. "He certainly didn't like it when I mentioned him."

"He's probably had to run off a number of other magicians trying to do what you're doing," said Ellory. She sat up straight and snapped her fingers. "The Enchantress! Perhaps that's why she was here!"

It made sense to Georgie. The Enchantress would have known enough Necromancy to do what he was about to attempt. "Maybe that is what disturbed the graveyard," said Georgie. "She tried and she couldn't."

Both of the children leapt out of their skins as a loud yowl sounded across the hills.

"Giant's teeth, what was that?" Ellory jumped to her feet, wielding her pen like a dagger.

A small, lithe shadow fell away from the shade in the woods. The Void had found them.

Georgie gulped as the cat approached. "What are you doing here?"

The Void meandered over in that special cat way of interested disdain. She sniffed the Enchantress's scarf on the ground, circled both children, and then rubbed against Georgie's leg.

"Do you think he sent her?" Ellory asked. "Is he spying on us through her eyes?"

Georgie considered the strong-willed cat rubbing against his leg with a jagged purr coming from her throat. "I don't think she'd let him."

The Void meowed in agreement, hopping onto the scarf and making herself at home in the center. She sniffed the open tome, her tail flicking in a way that to Georgie said, *"I'm here now. You may continue."*

Ellory kept a careful eye on the cat. "What did you need the book for if you simply wanted to talk to him?" she asked. "It sounds like you can already do that to some extent."

"I don't know," said Georgie, flipping through the pages. "I think I took it to make him mad."

"It doesn't seem smart to anger a Necromancer," said Ellory.

"No," agreed Georgie, flipping to the Incantation to Raise the Dead. "But it takes a little anger to get this far."

Chapter Twenty-Two

To resurrect a creature, so far as I have been able to, is a daunting task. To do so requires a mind to be split in two, a spectral heart and your own bloody organ to beat as one. It is disorienting. But with time and practice, I've been able to stretch the threads. Now, to resurrect a single undead is a mere tug on my subconscious mind. I cannot begin to stress how helpful this has been while pursuing my latest tutoring endeavors.

\- The Dying Art of Necromancy, *T.E.*

***

Georgie started to read. These runes were old, and he wasn't certain if he could pronounce them right. The script made him think of the sharp, jagged-peaked mountains and rumbling stone. He read the words silently once and twice, testing them one at a time on his tongue.

The Void poked her head curiously around Georgie's shoulder.

"You sound like a Necromancer," said Ellory, encouraging in her awe.

Georgie couldn't help but grin. "The pronunciation is the

hardest part, but I think I've got it. But the spell needs a name."

"How about 'Yoric'?" offered Ellory. "It should be safe enough."

There were more notes on the page, a list of emotions that the Necromancer had ticked off like a shopping list.

Amorous - Unacceptable

Joyful - Proving difficult

Desperation - Some promise

Anger - Finally.

But what was Georgie feeling?

The desperation was there. The need to get this right. And there was anger. Anger that the Necromancer had kept this from him, kept his mother away from him. After years of only having memories, the desire to have her by his side was far too strong to set aside now.

I have to bring her home, Georgie thought. *My mother needs to come home.*

He held on to that thought, clenching his fists tightly at his sides as if the action would hold his thought there. The desperate plea to whatever Necromantic magic lingered inside him to let him raise her up once more to life and bring his mother home.

The wind stopped, still and listening as Georgie began.

"Nouse pitkäuninen, Yoric. Vedä vielä kerran henkeä. Kutsukoon henkesi tuulesta, kehosi kivestä. Nouse! Herää! Olkoon se niin!"

There was a long pause of silence as the spell lingered in the air. Then nothing.

The Void gave a low meow. She was staring behind them at the hilltop, her hackles slowly rising.

Ellory sat back on her heels. "That sounded right to me. What does it mean?"

Georgie pointed to the different runes. "This is a command. This is a title of honor, and this—"

With a loud roar, the wind threw Georgie and Ellory onto their backs as it rushed towards the mountain. The air was a long, shuddering gasp, as if someone had been holding their breath for a long time.

Then the hillside erupted.

With a flash of purple, the Enchantress's scarf flew up off the ground, wrapping Georgie and Ellory in its silken embrace and pulling them out of harm's way. The tapestry flattened out beneath them, floating in midair with the children safely on its back. The curl of its corners reluctantly unwrapped them. Georgie grabbed the Void by the scruff of her neck, stuffing the loudly protesting cat into his shirt.

"A magic carpet!"

Georgie was glad Ellory could still voice her surprise. He seemed to have lost his. The scarf, now carpet, flew as fast as it could as the grassy surface of the hill broke open.

Large boulders, long buried beneath the earth, toppled down the mountainside as something underneath moved. They heard the gasp again as a dirt-encrusted mummified hand reached out from underground and grasped the edge.

The giant called Yoric rose from its grave.

The skin lay close to its bones, dried and mummified still after hundreds of years of death. Clumps of dirt clung to it in mounds of boulder and earth. The other hand joined it on either side, and with another lurch that made the whole mountainside sway beneath their feet, the giant sat up in its own grave.

"It's a giant," squeaked Ellory. "Georgie. It's a giant!"

Her voice sounded so distant from him—no, from the giant. The life thread stretched between Georgie and the giant, splitting his vision, his breath, and mind in two. He felt the giant's lungs, taking big, gulping breaths, while his own human heart fluttered wildly in his chest. Had the sun always been this bright? As if it could sense the sun, the giant shielded its eyes from the bright light. It was such a human motion, but with it, debris began to fall.

Georgie shouted in alarm as the carpet lurched, pulling them away from a tumbling stone. The Void screamed, furiously hissing and spitting at the giant towering above them.

"Put it back," said Ellory. "Georgie. Put it back!"

But Georgie didn't know how. The giant's thoughts tumbled across his own, flashes of sensation, and a sudden urgency in its bones. Too late, Georgie realized his error as the giant turned its face towards the village. Home. He had wanted his mother to go home.

The giant began to move.

The first step out of its grave rattled Georgie's teeth in his skull. The ground flattened beneath a massive, six-toed foot, the roots of this fifty-foot-tall creature. The giant didn't speak as it moved downhill, brushing aside the tall pine trees as if they were merely blades of grass.

"Georgie!" Ellory grabbed at his shirt, making him face her. "What did you do?"

Georgie frantically tried to put together what had happened, but his whole mind and being were consumed with panic, desperation, and fear at what he'd done. Each emotion flared like a bonfire hot in his chest. The footsteps of the giant picked up into its own panicked run, becoming a terrifying heartbeat that thundered in Georgie's ears.

Willing himself back to Earth, he pushed Ellory towards the front of the Enchantress's carpet and handed her the grimoire.

CHAPTER TWENTY-TWO

"We have to get closer!" With a flash of purple silk, the carpet flew off.

They raced on the carpet through the forest, glimpses of the giant's legs in between. The Void howled in Georgie's shirt as they raced down the mountainside. Even on top of the carpet, they could feel the reverberations of each step.

"Faster!" Ellory shouted, gripping the front ends of the carpet with everything she had, trying desperately to steer them clear of the falling debris.

Georgie's gaze was yanked upwards, the giant demanding sight to reach its ordered destination. It made it down the hill in little time at all, each stride a hundred more paces than Georgie's own. Everything seemed so small. The giant approached what appeared to be a child's dollhouse with red shingles faded from the sun. The garden to the side of the house was destroyed underneath a single footstep, vegetables squashed and splinters from the tidy fence flying into the air.

There was a loud shout, a mere squeak to the giant's distant ears as two people ran out onto the path outside. There was a flash of auburn hair, quickly covered by the bulk of the other person as he sheltered her from the falling debris.

Da. Aunt Elisa.

Back on the carpet, his own eyes blurring with tears, Georgie screamed.

"NO!"

The giant roared in an echo of its own, stumbling in its path and twisting itself violently to the side and smashing through the wooden gate towards the village. With the giant's gaze turned, Georgie lost sight of his family.

He felt his control on the giant slipping like sand through his trembling fingers. Were they all right? Had he hurt Aunt Elisa?

Were they even alive? Or were they buried beneath the rocks that had fallen from the giant?

This wasn't supposed to happen. He couldn't lose them. Not like this.

Distantly, he heard the Void yelling. Then he felt a sharp, sudden pain as she dug her sharp claws into his chest, pinning him back to his body.

"It's nearly reached the village!" Ellory shouted as the giant broke the tree line. Georgie could hear the distant screaming echoing in the giant's ears as it ran in full sight of the village.

Ellory directed the protesting tapestry closer. It nimbly darted out of the way of falling rock and rubble, pieces of the shattered rock leaping up towards them with ferocious speed. The giant stumbled over several houses, chimneys crumbling onto the streets below. The cobblestones split apart beneath its footfalls. The giant was in pain, confused and utterly terrified.

Georgie shouted up at the giant. "Stop! You have to stop!"

The giant was at the very edge of town now, smashing one of the wells underfoot as easily as an anthill. The firm step loosed the rubble from its body, falling down around Georgie and Ellory.

A large rock caught the edge of the carpet, throwing the children off of it. They rolled along the ground, gathering scrapes and cuts until they finally came to a stop. Georgie's ears rang from the impact, stars in his eyes mixing with coated dust. He landed on his back, all the breath knocked out of him. He felt his hair tugged forward as a loud crack of bright-blue lightning cut across the clear sky.

The Necromancer had arrived.

Hovering above the ground, standing on bolts of lightning in the center of the village square, the Necromancer was a veritable source of power as he faced the oncoming giant.

He started to chant, his voice cutting across the chaos as loud as cannon fire.

"KUOLLUT, ÄLÄ KÄVELE!"

With each flick of his wrists, the Necromancer's palms glowed with lightning before he thrust them towards the giant.

Bright-blue chains burst up from the ground. The first caught the giant's leg, then the next. The chains wrapped around the giant's body, jumping across its chest and pinning its arms to the side. With another sudden flash, the giant stood still, chained in place with its feet resting on the rubble of a villager's home.

Chapter Twenty-Three

Grief is the reaction to many losses. The loss of life is prominent in the human experience, but there are other losses. Alas, despite its many uses, Necromancy cannot mend the death of a relationship. That is a magic far beyond my own and is far too painful to pursue. This is the only death I will allow to exist, if only to save my own heart from the pain.

\- The Dying Art of Necromancy, *T.E.*

* * *

The townspeople crept forward as the Necromancer floated slowly to the ground.

"It's a giant!"

"What is it doing here?"

"Did you see? It came up out of the mountains!"

The Tombstone Mountains, still blissfully silent, took on a more awesome and intimidating light. They were graves. It was in the village's name. Why else would you need a Necromancer if not to guard the graves of sleeping giants from ages past?

The giant stood still, something twitching beneath its mummified eyelids as if it were looking about in confusion for why it had stopped. The breath in its lungs still rumbled in its chest.

"Are there more coming?"

"We should all leave! Now!"

The Void, still quaking with fear, released her clawed hold on Georgie's chest. She leapt out of his shirt and ran off into the shadows. With a groan, Georgie rolled over, pressing his head to the cobblestone street, promising to never leave the ground again. The Enchantress's tapestry wrestled itself from beneath the rubble, flying towards Georgie with the temperament of a sad puppy.

The Necromancer's shadow reached Georgie first.

Up till this moment, Georgie hadn't found the Necromancer particularly hard to read, but now his face was a blank slate, a carefully controlled mask that Georgie knew held back something terrible. The tapestry instinctually curled around his neck once more, shrinking back into the purple scarf.

The Necromancer held out his hand. Georgie reached to take it, but the Necromancer slapped it away. "The book, Georgie."

Ellory appeared beside him, both her knees scraped and bleeding. Standing ever so slightly in front of Georgie on the ground, she thrust the book towards the Necromancer.

The Necromancer snatched it away from her, rifling through the pages quickly. No doubt seeing that everything was in order, he gave a deep sigh and tucked the book beneath his robes as the crowd grew closer.

"Ellory? Georgie?" Aunt Elisa ran forward. The Necromancer barely stepped aside before she was there, wrapping the children up in a fierce embrace. "Oh, thank heavens you're safe!" She kissed both their cheeks, brushing the hair from their faces and then kissing them again.

The Necromancer stood awkwardly by, his lips pursed. His

only sign of annoyance.

"Wizard man." The Blacksmith held himself almost as still as the giant looming overheard. But he was not chained. He stepped very close to the Necromancer, keeping his voice low. "Did you do this? Did you endanger my son?"

Unlike before, the Necromancer did not cower in the Blacksmith's presence. He sniffed, holding his ground and raised his chin in defiance.

"Merely preventing further mistakes," the Necromancer answered. "The giant is harmless for the moment. But I will need to move him." His ice-blue eyes pierced Georgie to the core. "If you have further questions, I'm sure my apprentice will be able to assist."

The Blacksmith's head reared up in shock. "Son, did *you* do this?"

Ashamed, Georgie couldn't look at his father. Not after he'd nearly lost him and his aunt with one reckless spell. He struggled to nod, feeling the giant's electrically bound limbs humming in his own.

"Everyone, return to your homes!" the Priest said, his fellow clergy fanning out across the grounds to settle the rest. "Our wizard will set things right. The danger has passed."

"Come, Georgie," the Necromancer ordered.

Brave Aunt Elisa took Georgie by both shoulders, replacing the stony stare of the Necromancer with her warm brown eyes. "Are you all right?"

Georgie knew he couldn't leave a giant on the edge of town. They were bound together now, and only he could put it right. He would have to be. He nodded, forcing a smile.

Aunt Elisa frowned, clearly unbelieving, but stood all the same. "Brave boy."

The Blacksmith lingered, his hands clenched at his sides in a show of restraint. Aunt Elisa placed her hand on his chest, the ring glinting on her finger. "Wait, Alistair."

Carefully, Georgie stood by the Necromancer's side. He smelled sharp, like a lightning-struck tree. The Necromancer muttered a few words beneath his breath, the blue lightning energy flaring around his hands once more.

The chains around the giant did not loosen, but they did grow longer. They reminded Georgie of puppet strings. A vein bulged on the Necromancer's head as he concentrated, twitching his hands and fingers as he would a marionette. The entire village watched in muted awe as the giant turned on its heel and began marching back towards the mountains.

Georgie's legs moved with the giant's, hesitant, stiff, and afraid.

* * *

The walk up the mountain had never felt longer. The giant moved forward with awkward, shuffling steps, still bound by the chains. Its eyes turned in its head towards the village, still longing to fulfill Georgie's initial order.

"Calm your emotions, Georgie," the Necromancer ordered, gritting his teeth.

"Sir?"

"Your fear," he snapped back. "Control it."

But it was not as simple as the Necromancer wanted it to be. Georgie had to concentrate hard on the feeling in his chest, to linger in the overwhelming awfulness. He'd nearly gotten his entire family killed. Aunt Elisa, his da, even Ellory. The ache echoed in the giant overhead, whose own mind swirled with old memories and emotions that Georgie could barely put a name to. The bear had been easier, as its animal instincts had been more contained. But this giant spirit, clinging to its undead bones, overwhelmed him.

He pushed the giant aside, far away from his mind. It groaned overhead, as if the giant felt the distance of its master and regretted it. Georgie's mind and heart didn't feel any better. Now he only felt numb. Still, it seemed to work. The giant's limbs went lax, following the Necromancer's lead as meekly as Georgie.

They followed the giant's footsteps back to its resting place, now a gaping crater with downtrodden trees and broken rock.

"Let it go," the Necromancer instructed.

Georgie shied back. "I…I don't know how."

"If you do not, it will fall on top of us. You've done it once before. Figure it out."

Georgie felt like he was about to cry while the giant's eyes blinked furiously as it held back its own.

"There is a tether," the Necromancer explained. "Like a thread in your chest tied to this being. Find it in your soul. Find peace with it. Let it go."

Georgie closed his eyes, pausing his trembling to prod his heart.

Letting go was harder than expected. He wanted nothing to do with this giant anymore. He wanted to be free from his failure more than anything. But this giant was alive. The memories of its own life swirled overtop his own. Memories of a roaring bonfire, the deep rumbling laughter of its kin, and the joy of having the warmth of the sunlight on its face. The giant was confused why the world looked so different now and why everyone seemed so small. Yet despite the confusion, there was an innocent curiosity. The giant wanted to live to find out more.

It was precious to him, this giant. His desire had come alive, and to let it go meant that he would have to see that dream die. Georgie knew, as deep as his bones, that he would never be allowed near any sort of Necromancy again after this. It was little wonder the Death-Weaver had been sundered while he'd been tied to so many beings.

"Georgie," the Necromancer warned. "*Now.*"

He didn't let go so much as tear it loose. He grasped the thread wrapped around his heart and pulled it away, gasping as a wave of loss hit him. Georgie had never felt so small and lost.

The giant slumped forward, groaning as it fell, as heavy and final as an ancient tree. The Necromancer winced, his arms straining to hold it. He muttered, more chanting through gritted teeth. The giant caught itself in midair, but the life that Georgie had given it was gone.

The Necromancer laid the giant back down in its grave. Like a child playing in the sand, the giant's body gathered up the rock and dirt around it, slowly burying itself once more. The last of the sun's rays disappeared behind the mountain as the giant finally sank fully beneath the earth. The ground rose and sank as the giant gave its last breaths. It slowed and then finally grew still.

The Necromancer's arms fell wearily to his sides, his brow coated with sweat. His lightning-blue eyes flickered to Georgie. "This will be your final lesson."

Georgie swallowed the lump in his throat. "Yes, sir."

"After the Death-Weaver fell, the King made a decree. It frightened him that even a dead giant could be such a force for destruction. As such, both he and the Council of Magi decreed a Necromancer should always be stationed here. For centuries, this has been the case. My mentor, Sardis, was the caretaker before me." The Necromancer gave a long sigh. "And I shall be the last."

"I am sorry, sir," said Georgie.

The Necromancer nodded to himself. "You should be. Now go. Don't bother coming back."

Without another word, Georgie limped down the path towards home. With the giant gone, his body recognized its own long list of hurts. Spots of blood speckled the front of his shirt, and he could feel the knot on his head swell. He tugged at the Enchantress's scarf, but the magic remained dormant, rejecting him just as the Necromancer had.

But then he heard his father's voice.

"Georgie?" The Blacksmith stood in the middle of the road, his face creased with worry.

The tears which Georgie had held for so long came bursting forth in aching sobs. He ran towards his father, falling into the Blacksmith's strong embrace.

"It's all right, son," his father murmured softly, holding him as close as he could. "It's all right."

The Blacksmith scooped up Georgie in his arms like a babe, and for the first time in many years, he carried his son home.

Chapter Twenty-Four

I cannot show the boy how to bring his mother back to life. Not now. She would be a monster, a shell of the woman who was clearly loved by her family. He doesn't realize it yet, but he has already created a shell of her in his mind. He's filled up this portrait of what he thinks all should be. There is not one person who can solve the problem of grief. No matter how much magic they may possess.

 - The Dying Art of Necromancy, *T.E.*

***

It was dark by the time Georgie and his father had made it home. Aunt Elisa greeted them at the door with a warm fire in the hearth and the kettle whistling gently on the stove. Ellory sat sheepishly on the edge of the table next to a bowl of red-tinted water and a pile of bandages. Her chin was patched up with a neat row of stitches, and her legs were wrapped in white gauze.

The Blacksmith's chest rumbled against Georgie's ear. "Elisa, would you mind if I...?"

"Not at all," she murmured, squeezing the Blacksmith's arm. She had her own scratch across her brow but looked more weary than injured. "Are you all right to walk, Ellory? It's time we headed home."

Ellory, unusually quiet and demure, gave a nod as she slid off the table. Aunt Elisa kept her arms wrapped protectively around her daughter as she shut the door behind them.

The Blacksmith gently lowered Georgie down in a chair in front of the fire. "Take off your shirt, son."

Georgie winced as he peeled it away, revealing the angry marks the Void had left. The Blacksmith refilled the bowl on the table with steaming water, gathering up the clean bandages Aunt Elisa had set aside. He knelt in front of Georgie, brushing the hair from his son's eyes. "This might sting."

While the Blacksmith carefully cleaned Georgie's wounds, Georgie found that he couldn't look at his father. He didn't want to see what further disappointment or anger he would hold for him.

But when the Blacksmith finally did speak, it was a quiet question. "Why did you do it, Georgie?"

"It was an accident," he murmured, his head still lowered. "I didn't mean to. I was trying…"

"Trying to do what?"

Georgie grimaced. "Did you know the wizard was a Necromancer?"

The Blacksmith grunted in his chest. "I've heard the rumors. I took little notice of them, but clearly, I should have. But why Necromancy, Georgie? Of all things?"

Georgie had never felt so small. "I wanted to bring back Mum." He rushed to explain as the Blacksmith sat back on his heels in surprise. "You've been so sad for so long, and it frightens me. I'm afraid you'll leave again, and I don't want you to."

The Blacksmith was a good listener. He always had been, even if Georgie hadn't stumbled upon the words until now. The firelight flickered in his patient gaze, steady and true.

"I know I can't help at the forge," said Georgie. "And with Aunt Elisa here, I can't help with the house as much. But I want to help. I want you to not have to be so sad all the time. And I thought…" Georgie wrestled with the thread of truth as he had with the giant. "I thought you might be angry with me if I found a way to bring her back and didn't."

The Blacksmith was quiet as he got to his feet. He pulled up another chair from the table in front of the fire and sat in it with a weary sigh.

"You are right, son," he said. "I have been lost in my grief for many years and have been holding on to your mother far longer than I should have. For years after her death, I thought something might have happened to her. That there'd been someone responsible for it and if I could find them, everything would make sense. The anger was powerful and as hot as my own forge. I desperately wanted someone to blame, and often it was myself. I withdrew then because as much as I wanted someone to blame, the only person I could find to blame was myself."

The Blacksmith spoke as if he were presenting a finished piece of ironwork. It was rough on some edges, sharp on others, while some words still lingered with a fiery glow of emotion. It was whole, in a way that made Georgie realize his father hadn't been lost in his grief all these years, but simply working his way out of it as best he'd known how.

"Part of my hesitation in you learning magic was because of your mother. I worried that if you learned how capable you are with it, that it might draw you away." The Blacksmith blinked several times. "Today, it nearly did." He cleared his throat twice before he continued. "The night that she died…she told me she 'felt something was wrong.' A feeling that sent her up into the hills towards the dead wizard's house despite him having been gone for months. I couldn't stop her, but I wonder if I tried hard enough to." The Blacksmith's lips twitched with a bittersweet smile. "Though nothing would have worked when her mind was set on something."

The Blacksmith sat back in his chair. "But then Old Woodsman died. Suddenly someone else was gone in the same unexplainable way, which is when I realized that there wasn't anyone to blame. People die, sometimes in unexpected ways. No matter how much we love them.

"That's when I realized that I needed to let go. In hanging on to that grief, that anger, I twisted the memory of your mother. I twisted it until I couldn't remember the better times. She became something to me that wasn't what she would ever have wanted. I was forgetting what was important."

The Blacksmith gripped Georgie's shoulder. "You're important to me, Georgie. Our family here, as small as it is. And Elisa… She has become important to me. Both her and Ellory in their own special ways."

Georgie twisted his discarded shirt in his hands. "Sometimes I feel like I never knew Mum and that all she does is take those I love away from me because she's gone. When you got engaged, I knew I wouldn't be able to bring Mum back if everyone had moved on."

"And what do you think now?"

"I love Aunt Elisa," said Georgie. "I don't know if I love her more than Mum, but it feels fuller somehow. Is that wrong?"

The Blacksmith shook his head. "No, son. Your mother would

have wanted someone to care for you if she could not. And I can think of no better person than Elisa. Can you?"

That brought a smile to Georgie's lips. "I don't think so."

The Blacksmith took Georgie's hands in his own, gripping them tightly. "If I've learned anything, it's that grief and anger don't go away on their own. But if you're able to let it go, new things can spring up. It's good to mourn the loss of a loved one. It means that they mattered. I'm sorry that I left you for it. I should have been there to care for you, and I wasn't. And I ask your forgiveness for not being able to speak with you about it until now."

It was as if the warmth of the fire had finally seeped into Georgie's very bones. The threads of emotions untangled in his chest, and he could finally breathe. "I forgive you."

The Blacksmith bowed his head. "Thank you. Perhaps together, we can build something new. With Elisa and Ellory." He leaned in, now a playful conspirator. "You're the only one who knows this, but I'm nervous about it, too. It's been a long time with just the two of us. But despite how nervous I am, perhaps this change will be less frightening than Necromancy?"

Georgie wholeheartedly agreed.

* * *

The following week was relatively silent from all forms of Necromancy. Georgie stuck close to the house at his father's insistence to heal and recover. Georgie spent many an hour at his window seat, watching the rest of the villagers clean up the mess he'd made. Far too often, his eyes would drift past back towards the mountains, expecting them to move on their own again.

Georgie was left to wonder what the Necromancer was doing all alone in his cottage on the hill. He missed the routine of his lessons, the scent of magic in the air, and even Herbert's lectures. More than anything, he missed how capable he'd felt with magic thrumming in his hands. He understood now why his mother had continued to help Sardis in exchange for magic lessons.

But the Necromancer had made it clear that Georgie would never touch Necromancy again. He only had to look outside at the giant footprint, still in the center of his aunt's garden, to remind himself why.

To say that the villagers of Yoricsgrave were unnerved was an understatement. Some of the wealthier population left, hoping that the larger cities would hold fewer earthquakes. Even Aunt Elisa's snooty employer, Mrs. Havershem, was quick to flee to the safety of her summer home. But not everyone in Yoricsgrave was as flighty. Indeed, many of the villagers, the Blacksmith included, were as solid as stone itself. The village returned to daily life slowly, moving on past what they couldn't control to what they could. Market days, herding sheep, and working with iron.

With Mrs. Havershem no longer an issue, preparations for the Blacksmith and Aunt Elisa's wedding went unhindered. Georgie helped tidy up the house, making space in the long-empty rooms for Ellory and helping Aunt Elisa arrange what little she'd brought with her just so.

"We could go away for a few nights," Aunt Elisa said shyly at dinner. "Not for long, of course, but perhaps to the next village over?"

The Blacksmith's brow furrowed. "And the children?"

"They'll be all right. We'll leave plenty of food and have

CHAPTER TWENTY-FOUR

Callum check up on them."

"We won't get into trouble," said Georgie. "You should go."

Ellory didn't make promises she couldn't keep, and she settled on a wide smile. "We'll be fine!"

The Blacksmith made a disbelieving noise in his chest in reluctant agreement.

The wedding was a simple early-autumn celebration. It was quiet, as the Blacksmith had requested. The Village Priest stood with Georgie and his father, with but a few well-wishing villagers to line the aisle. Per Aunt Elisa's request, there were flowers everywhere. The sweet scent lingered in the air. A myriad of flower petals covered the entire aisle, drifting as lazily as fireflies in the mountain breeze.

The Blacksmith shifted on his feet as they waited at the front, nervously tugging at his necktie. Georgie himself felt smartly dressed in his own new waistcoat and shining shoes. His nose itched a bit from all the flowers, but he didn't mind. He gently tugged his father's sleeve to lower his hand. "Here they come."

Aunt Elisa glowed in her simple white frock, her hands overflowing with an enormous bouquet of sunflowers and bright-red poppies. Ellory walked proudly beside her mother, in a bright-red dress and with her hair covered with a sunflower crown.

The vows were simple and heartfelt. Ellory and Georgie grinned as the Blacksmith cleared his throat for the third time while reciting them. However, the gruff exterior of the Blacksmith melted away as Aunt Elisa lovingly brushed away the tears from his cheek.

The celebration afterward was a blur of happiness. Georgie ate until he was stuffed then ate again after Ellory had run him ragged from dancing. He'd never seen his father smile so much nor heard Aunt Elisa laugh as brightly. When food and drink had settled and even the most tireless villagers had wandered back home, the new family went to the graveyard.

"I feel a bit like a ghost," said Aunt Elisa. "Wandering out here in white on my wedding day. Whatever will the gossips think?"

The Blacksmith held her hand, a new gold band on his ring finger to match hers. "Nothing of importance."

They reached the marble gravestone beneath the willow tree. The sun was setting beyond the hills, dabbling through the leaves like stained glass.

Aunt Elisa laid her wedding bouquet by her sister's grave. "I miss you," she said. "And I love you still. I pray you know that, darling. I'm so grateful for all that you've done for me, even now."

Ellory set her flower crown on the top of the gravestone. "Love you, Auntie."

The Blacksmith placed his hand on the stone, caressing it as softly as he might have his first wife in life. His voice was low and soft, only for her. "Thank you. For always."

Georgie took a deep breath. It was time. He knelt down in front of his mother's grave as the rest of his family drifted back, graciously giving him a moment alone.

"I guess this is goodbye," said Georgie. "It feels real this time. Now that I know how dangerous it is, I won't be trying to bring you back. I hope you can forgive me for that."

The gravestone didn't answer, and for once, Georgie was thankful for it.

"Without you, I wouldn't be here," he continued. "I wouldn't have known Ellory or Elisa. Da might never have found his happiness again if it weren't for them."

Georgie traced his mother's inscription one last time. "I miss you," he confessed. "Even if it isn't the same way that the others do, it's true. But maybe instead of trying hard to be as sad as everyone around me, I'll try harder to be happy. I think that's what you would have wanted."

His father's hand rested gently on his shoulder. "It's time, son."

Georgie nodded. "Goodbye, Mum. Rest well."

Chapter Twenty-Five

To raise an undead, destroy it again, and then hope the soul returns another time is a risky business. Better to keep it animated for as long as possible. This requires constant attention and due diligence. It is exhausting to say the least, but the consequences for failure are far worse. I will sleep when I am dead. If I am successful, I will never see death at all.

\- The Dying Art of Necromancy, *T.E.*

* * *

The children wished their parents farewell at dusk, promising to take care of the house and await their return. The new husband and wife walked hand in hand towards the waiting coach, disappearing down the road just as the cloudless sky had turned dark.

The rain came heavily, pattering on the windows of the house with rapid insistence. Georgie had gone to bed early but was awake now, lying in the dark of his room to listen as the wind howled outside. He rolled over, putting his back to the window to try to fall back asleep. He was just drifting off when he noticed something odd.

The flashes of lightning were blue.

Georgie immediately sat up in bed as the thunder cracked over the house, rattling it down to its wooden bones. Stumbling out of bed, he pressed his nose to the glass of his window. The darkness was nearly absolute but for the lonely lantern that sputtered valiantly at the gate.

The flashes of blue lightning were there again. Flashing once, twice, each separate from the thunder that followed from nature's own storm. There was one last magnificent *CRACK!* before even the storm itself fell silent.

And then, there was an angry yowl outside.

Georgie nearly leapt out of his skin at the sheer rage of it, stumbling downstairs despite wanting to run the other way as the yowling continued, over and over. He opened the door as fast as he could, letting the soaked, furious cat inside.

"Void? What are you doing here?"

The black cat shook herself in the entryway, spattering Georgie with cold rainwater. She shook one paw, then the other, and then her back feet, still growling beneath her breath as she wandered over to the dying embers of the fire.

Georgie carefully approached the sodden cat, grabbing one of the dish towels from the kitchen. "What happened out there?" He knelt down next to her, holding the towel out to her. "Where's the Necromancer?"

The Void paused her insistent grooming to look up at him with her large green eyes. She gave a low meow. Then, to the surprise of them both, the Void walked into the towel and allowed herself to be dried off.

The oddness of the night continued when the Void refused to leave. After a dish of sardines and a few more towels, she took herself upstairs and made herself at home on Georgie's bed. She yelled at him when he tried to ask more questions, only settling when he was back in bed himself.

The rumbling in his room was different now as the Void purred them both to sleep.

The next morning, the Void was still there. Like an ink stain on his bedsheets, she lay in a perfect circle at the foot of Georgie's bed. The sky outside remained overcast, but the amount of rain had fallen to a drizzle.

The Void noticed the moment he tried to slip away. She popped one green eye open.

"I'm just going downstairs," said Georgie.

The Void stood up, stretching her back in an arch, and hopped off the bed to lead the way.

It was as they were both sitting down for breakfast, oatmeal for Georgie and a small saucer of cream for the Void, when Callum banged on the door.

"Georgie? Ellory? Is everyone all right?"

The Void hissed at the intrusion, but Georgie batted her away long enough to open it. The young Blacksmith looked relieved to see him.

"Giant's blessed rest, you're safe."

"We're fine," Georgie said, letting him in. "But what happened? Was it the storm?"

"You could say that," he replied, looking about the house as if he expected something to leap out at them.

"Morning, Callum." Ellory's sleepy voice sounded from the stairwell. She was dressed, but her brown hair was still a tangled bird's nest around her head. She rubbed at her eyes with a yawn. "What storm?"

Georgie couldn't help but grin. Ellory had slept through it

all.

"There was a storm, yes," said Callum. "But more than that. Folks say that they saw blue lightning and heard sounds of some sort of commotion from the east. Then this morning, the Priest comes running in and says something's happened at the graveyard. I don't know what, but it's not—"

Ellory perked up immediately. She grabbed a piece of bread from the counter, her bag from the doorknob, and burst out the door before Callum could stop her. "Georgie, come on!"

The Blacksmith looked at Georgie, who could only shrug and follow her out the door.

* * *

The graveyard was in shambles. Broken gravestones littered the churchyard. There were toppled memorial spires, while other more modest stones were shorn in half by some immense force. Scorch marks lingered on the ground near them, and some of the oldest trees were now smoldering ruins.

There was a large group of people in the center, a mix of priests, the nervous gravedigger, and the bright-purple form of the Enchantress flitting among them like a butterfly.

Ellory didn't seem to be interested in asking questions, but Georgie needed to know. His cousin ran in the opposite direction as he walked down the hill, the Void following close on his heels.

As he grew closer towards the main group, he saw the bones.

Fragments of femurs, skull shards, and an entire skeletal arm jutted out from the dirt in the churchyard. It reminded Georgie a little of the earlier battle, except this time, it had been between skeletons alone.

"I've never seen anything like this," said the Enchantress, her elegant voice filled with concern. "And he didn't say anything to you at all?"

The Priest shook his head. "Nothing. I only heard his spells and the voice of another flinging them back at him. He must have drawn the Creature off."

"Is the Necromancer all right?" Georgie asked.

The Priest and the Enchantress both turned to the boy. The two adults exchanged a look before the Priest gave a nod to dismiss himself.

"Hello, Georgie," said the Enchantress. "It doesn't seem that way, does it?"

"I thought you'd left town," he said.

"I did. Until a little bird caught up to me on the road and called me back." She shook her head at the destruction. "I don't know what to make of this. Has he said anything to you?"

Georgie squirmed. "No. He...He doesn't want to teach me anymore."

The Enchantress frowned. "But you show so much promise!"

"I made a mistake. A big one."

The Enchantress hummed in her throat. "He's hardly one to judge now, is he?"

Georgie startled as the Void pressed herself between his shins, wrapping her tail around one of his legs. She sniffed at the air but stayed close.

"Hello, Void," said the Enchantress.

The Void hissed back.

Georgie nudged the cat with his leg. "Sorry about that."

"Don't be," said the Enchantress with a small laugh. "She's the only creature who isn't fond of me. It's refreshing. How long has she been with you?"

CHAPTER TWENTY-FIVE

"She showed up last night," Georgie explained. "She won't leave, either."

The Enchantress raised a single elegant brow. "I don't suppose you'll tell me more, will you, Void?"

The cat flicked her ears back and meowed a very clear *"No."*

The Enchantress rolled her eyes. "Typical. Keep your secrets then, cat. But if you are here and Tristan is not, that doesn't bode well." She patted Georgie on the shoulder. "Stay safe and don't worry. I'll take care of it."

"Yes, ma'am," Georgie replied as the Enchantress floated away. He looked down at the Void between his feet. "You could have been more polite."

The Void ignored this, bending down to lick her paws.

Georgie jostled the frustrating cat as he stepped away. "Come on. We'd better find Ellory."

He didn't have to look far. While the rest of the adults were busy in the yard, Ellory was at the entrance to Kaspar's mausoleum with crowbar in hand.

"What are you doing?" Georgie gasped after his run up the hill.

"I have a theory," she said, opening the still-unlocked door with a loud creak.

"We can't be in here!" he exclaimed, even as they walked through the door. "Not again!"

His cousin didn't seem the least bit perturbed. She marched straight up to the obsidian sarcophagus in the center of the room. "Oh, hush, Georgie, and lend me a hand."

Georgie shook his head wildly. "No. No, I'm not helping you. The Necromancer nearly bit my head off when I even *suggested* talking to Kaspar."

"You don't have to talk to him, Georgie," said Ellory, gritting her teeth as she shoved the lid. "Besides…" The coffin lid fell to the ground with a heavy *thud*. "He's not even here."

The coffin of Kaspar Cynward, the Death-Weaver, lay empty.

Chapter Twenty-Six

The flaws of the resurrected dead are obvious. They are decaying corpses. They cannot eat, drink, or live as a mortal ought to. They are simply filled with whatever their maker desires for them. No soul, living or alive, should be under such torment.

\- The Dying Art of Necromancy, T. E.

* * *

The Enchantress's face paled enough to rival the dead when she discovered them.

"How long have you known about this?" she demanded.

Ellory twirled the crowbar in her hands, a satisfied grin on her face. "A couple of weeks," she said. "Or at least that it was open. But then the Necromancer said, 'No one is in there,' and it made me think."

"The Necromancer? You were here with Tristan?"

Georgie quickly stepped in. "Not exactly."

The Enchantress looked back and forth at both of them before closing her eyes and taking a deep, calming breath.

The Priest and Groundskeeper Bron entered behind her with several lanterns, lighting up the carvings inside. Kaspar's death mask on the far wall stared down at them with unseeing eyes. With the extra light, the threads spinning out from his hands glowed with a flicker of fool's gold.

"He was sealing the oldest graves, mistress," said the Priest thoughtfully. "For residual Necromantic magic."

"He offered to do the same with the rest that were buried," said the Groundskeeper. "When I pressed him, he merely said that it was a precaution."

"Yes, well, the undead body of the Death-Weaver would certainly hold enough residual magic to do such a thing," said the Enchantress, her elegant calm quickly fading. "If the mess outside is anything to go by, it might not be all that residual anymore."

"That's amazing!" said Ellory before Georgie could clamp his hand over her mouth.

The Enchantress pointedly ignored her. "How long has he been sealing the gravesites?" asked the Enchantress.

"I think the first was perhaps six or seven years ago when he first arrived," said the Priest. "What would you say, Bron?"

"Aye, sir," the Groundskeeper agreed. "Ever since the incident with the Smith's wife."

Georgie felt the air snatched from his lungs. "Adelaide? Adelaide Smith was the first he sealed?" Had he seen the Necromancer there all those years ago? The memories were infuriatingly dim in his mind, crowded by the rush of questions.

"I think it's the time the children were sent back home," said the Priest quietly.

Ellory protested. "But we—"

"Come on, Ellory," Georgie said, his own voice seeming to echo within his ears. "It's time to go."

He led the Void and a still-grumbling Ellory back home, barely registering her complaints as they walked. What did it all mean? Why had the Necromancer sealed his mother's grave first? Was that the reason he was so adamantly against bringing her back? He didn't have answers, simply an empty grave and a mentor who didn't want him.

They found Callum at their house when they arrived.

"I'll be staying the night tonight," he promised. "Just downstairs if you need me. At least until your parents are home."

"Thanks, Callum," said Georgie.

Unfazed by the surrounding nerves, Ellory impatiently beckoned Georgie up the stairs towards her room. "It didn't make sense until you told me about the Death-Weaver," she said. "That's when it all fell into place."

Georgie had made sure that Ellory's new room was sparkling clean and neat in a way that was welcoming. He couldn't hide his gasp when she opened the door and revealed what she'd done with the place.

Scraps of paper were pinned to the entire length of the eastern wall. Some of them were sketches, others were bits of newspaper clippings, and many of them were pieces of Ellory's journal that had been ripped out and kept here. They were all connected by various threads of mismatched string.

Her bed had been shoved to the side to make more room, as some of the dangling ends of string were reaching around the corner of it and around the window. It reminded Georgie of a cluttered spiderweb. The Void stepped in behind them, heading straight to the pile of blankets on the bed for a nap.

Ellory marched straight up to the wall and pointed to a piece of paper with the words 'Death-Weaver' written on it. She tapped at it insistently before following what was clearly part of Georgie's old shoelaces towards another paper. "Kaspar

Cynward is on the loose."

Georgie sat down on Ellory's bed, his jaw still open in shock. "What?"

The Void protested at being jostled but settled when Georgie reached out to gently stroke her midnight-black fur.

Ellory turned on her heel towards Georgie, her face lit up with glee. "I think the Necromancer has been trying to capture him."

"Ellory…" Georgie shook his head. "That's…"

"Look, though!" She ran back to her board. "The Old Woodsman dies from an attack from an animal, but it can't have been one that he'd seen before because he wasn't prepared. Next up, the Necromancer commissions your da to make chains. Special ones, with lots of runes. Third…" She pointed to a stick drawing with bright-red hair. "He takes you on as his apprentice. I think he offered to tutor you so that you could help him."

"Something released Kaspar from his grave," said Ellory as she paced back and forth. "Maybe it was his old mentor, Sardis. Or perhaps he's always been wandering the hills. We don't know how long the mausoleum has been empty because no one bothered to look! At first, I thought the Enchantress might have raised him, but she's too nice. You saw her. She walked around the whole graveyard today, and her magic affected nothing. Whatever is causing that effect has to be something older and more powerful, and who could that possibly be besides the First Necromancer?"

"This is a lot," said Georgie, still trying to wrap his mind around it all.

"It is," Ellory agreed proudly.

"But…what are we going to do about this?" Georgie asked.

"What do you mean? We can do a lot!" Ellory bounced over to

him. "I think the Creature, what was once Kaspar, is hiding in the woods. It's possible that he'll be drawn to magic. Specifically, *your* magic. That's why he chased us in the graveyard that night."

"I didn't do any magic that night," said Georgie.

"No," said Ellory. "But you have training. If anyone could sense it, Kaspar would. If we can lure the Creature out, perhaps lead it straight to the Necromancer, then he can—"

"Is *this* why you asked me to share my notes?" Georgie asked, interrupting. "So that you could figure all this out?"

Ellory winced. "Sort of."

Georgie took in all of Ellory's notes. The Old Woodsman's death, his father's commission, and the empty mausoleum. There were the things that she hadn't seen, like the notes throughout the Necromancer's book, or the tower room that was kept as cold as death itself despite the sunlight. She was thorough, he'd give her that, but there was still something missing, one final piece that lay hidden in the shadows so deep that even Ellory in all her brightness couldn't uncover it. Georgie wasn't sure if he wanted to go further into the dark to find it.

"The Necromancer needs our help," said Ellory. "We can do this!"

"Ellory, this is amazing," he said softly. "But he doesn't want my help anymore. He made that very clear."

"But *want* and *need* are different things," she said.

Georgie shook his head. "We can't. Let's ask Callum to send word to the Enchantress. We can show her all of this and see what she can do about it. She's the one trained in magic, after all."

Ellory's face crumbled with disappointment. "But...we're so close!"

"I'm sorry, Ellory," he said, getting up to leave. "But I'm done with Necromancy."

* * *

The rain returned that night with a vengeance. Georgie lay awake for hours, tossing and turning in his bed, with images of Ellory's wall flashing like lightning in his memory.

"He needs your help," Ellory had said. But if that were true, then why had he sent him away? The Enchantress was the only hope of fixing this, but hadn't the Necromancer also shoved her aside? Images of the Necromancer fighting off a horde of skeletons, only to be buried beneath them, rattled through Georgie's mind.

He couldn't remember falling asleep, with all his questions swirling in his mind.

Then the Void screamed in his face.

He startled awake. The black cat's green eyes and a flash of sharp teeth glowed in the faint light of the lantern outside. Her claws dug into his chest as she yowled again.

"What?" Georgie practically fell out of bed. "What's going on?"

The Void meowed again, leaping off of the bed and heading out the door. Surely she didn't want to be let out now in this storm.

Callum lay in the sitting room downstairs, stretched across the couch with an old quilt overtop him. The young man snored lightly, dead to the world and the thunderstorm outside. Georgie kept quiet, following the insistent Void to the door. He reached for his oilskin where it hung from the wall.

Ellory's oilskin was missing. The Void pawed at the row of

shoes, meowing again at the empty spot where Ellory's boots should have been. The empty spaces filled Georgie with dread, and a sliver of cold stroked down his entire spine.

Ellory was gone. Worse still, Georgie knew exactly where she was.

"Callum!" Georgie shouted, grabbing his own shoes. "Callum, wake up!"

"What?" the man asked, rubbing at his eyes. "What's wrong?"

"Get the Enchantress," said Georgie, throwing his oilskin over his head before grabbing a lantern and the Enchantress's scarf. "I have to find Ellory!"

"Georgie? Georgie, wait!"

But he was already running into the night and towards the hills. In between the rainclouds, the light of the sickle moon flickered down. Georgie kept his lantern close, praying beneath his breath that the flame would hold. The Void trotted at his heels, urging him on.

The Necromancer's cottage was dark when he arrived. There wasn't even an ember's glow peering out from the windows. The stone house endured the rain, as silent and still as a tombstone itself.

But the tower had fallen. Georgie guessed that whatever precarious fault line it had stood upon had been disrupted by the giant's resurrection. The top half of the tower had fallen off, leaving a jutting spire. The door lay on the ground, tossed aside in a mix of splinters and broken hinges.

With no help to be found, Georgie started yelling at the edge of the woods. "Ellory! Ellory, where are you?" But the wind lifted his voice away, spattering it back at him with the cold rain. The Void pawed at his leg, signaling him to follow before she led the way into the dark abyss of the woodlands.

He walked for what felt like hours, stumbling his way over jutting roots and thick pools of mud. He kept his voice to a whisper. "Ellory? Ellory, are you here?"

The Void stopped in front of him, her ears twitching for a moment. The cat gave a low growl in her throat before darting off to the right.

"Void! Wait!" Georgie ran after her into the brush.

A hand grabbed at his oilskin, yanking him down into the dirt. Before he could cry out, another clammy, wet hand pressed against his mouth.

"Quiet," Ellory hissed against his ear. When he complied, she snatched the lantern from his hand and blew out the light.

"What are you—?"

"Shush," said Ellory. He couldn't see her without the light, but she grabbed his hand. She was shivering. "It'll hear you."

The sharp cold from the tower struck Georgie in the chest. The smell of rot and decay hit his nostrils first, before the clanking of chains against bone followed. He clamped his mouth shut, desperate to keep his chattering teeth from giving them away. Stepping out from the shadows of the trees, a slender, human-like figure shuffled forward.

It was sniffing. Quick breaths in succession before it gave out a low moan that made Georgie's stomach roil with fear. The Creature reached out its arms in front of it, almost blindly feeling its way through the woods.

"What do we do?" Ellory whispered, crushing Georgie's hand in evident fear as the Creature's head twitched at the sound.

The answer was simple but no less terrifying. He would not allow it to harm Ellory.

"I'll draw it off," he replied. "Run and don't look back!" He didn't give her time to argue as he leapt to his feet. "Hey! Skull

CHAPTER TWENTY-SIX

Face! Over here!"

The Creature's head snapped towards him, and it lunged forward with an unnatural speed.

"Georgie, no!" Ellory shouted.

But he was already gone, and the Creature was following.

The forest stretched before him like an endless cavern of pitch black. The loam beneath his feet was slippery with the rain, while the roots of the trees seemed to stretch forward to trip him. Still, Georgie ran. The Creature's shuffling was wickedly fast behind him. It crashed through the branches, unhindered by anything that lay in its path.

"Georgie!" Ellory screamed in the darkness.

He didn't have time to see if the Creature was following him. Not if Ellory was in danger.

As he ran towards her voice, Georgie felt something tugging on his heart like a compass. The feeling guided him forward, straight as an arrow. There was a new sound beside him, and flickering in the darkness, Georgie saw a stag.

No, it was *the* stag, the one from the Enchantress. The mighty beast ran beside him, guiding him forward, with a spark of purple magic lingering in his eyes.

Together, they ran until Georgie broke through the tree line, teetering on the edge of a shale cliff. His arms flailed in the air before he regained his footing. His heart pounding in his chest, he looked around wildly.

"Ellory!" he shouted. "Ellory, where are you?"

Georgie had never been so happy to hear the Void's angry scream in reply.

The Void stood near Ellory, who lay slumped on the ground, covered in mud from head to toe. She lay distressingly still. Georgie fell to his knees beside her, grabbing her face with his hands. "Ellory? Ellory, wake up!" His hands came away slick with blood. "Giant's teeth." She must have fallen and slipped on the rocks. She'd been lucky she hadn't fallen over the cliffside.

The Void hissed behind him, yowling at the top of her lungs against the rain. Georgie's breath froze in the air in front of him as the bone-deep chill of the Creature's presence returned.

It was the first time that Georgie could properly see Kaspar, out here in the open with the moonlight flickering valiantly through the clouds. A robe of faded black and gray lay in tatters over its six-foot-tall frame, fluttering around the Creature like a ghost itself. The Creature had long since lost its nose, flattened and decayed with time. It was more of a skull than a face. Gaping black eyes stared out at Georgie, empty and soulless. Deep-running grooves ran over the Creature's arms, legs, and face as if the Creature had been tied so tightly that whatever held it remained pressed into its brittle and mummified flesh.

He had to do something. Now.

"Kuollut, älä…"

The Creature's head snapped to attention as Georgie chanted.

"Kuollut, älä käve…el…" His teeth were chattering, the Creature's presence a sharp and painful cold. The Creature shuffled forward, raising its arms out in front of it in an almost-desperate plea.

Georgie shut his eyes tightly. "Kuollut, älä kävele!" An electric hum gathered in his palms. "Kuollut, älä kävele!" He thrust out his hands in front of him and shouted, "KUOLLUT, ÄLÄ KÄVELE!"

With a flash of bright blue, lightning flew from Georgie's hands. The Creature was struck in the chest, wailing as the magical chains wrapped around its shrieking form. A chain for each leg, another around its chest to bind its arms.

With one final moan, the Creature was still.

Chapter Twenty-Seven

I've delved into these studies for far longer than any student before me. My ambition has driven me this far. I could have stayed in the city with my peers, followed a different pursuit of magic, and found happiness. Morgan always tells me this, offering other spells and passions like brightly colored sweets. But I chose my path long ago, and when I am successful, Necromancy will end. It will never be needed again.

  - The Dying Art of Necromancy, *T.E.*

* * *

The Creature stood, bound, still and close enough that Georgie's misty gasps faded over its undead face. It tilted its head to the side, reminding Georgie of a wounded puppy. Feeling the electric tether between them still holding, Georgie risked returning to Ellory. His cousin groaned on the ground, unconscious but still alive.

"Void," he said to the cat, who wisely kept her gaze on the Creature behind him, "can you run and find the Necromancer?"

The cat gave a low meow, her tail twitching side to side as

the shadows lengthened and the Necromancer appeared as if summoned by his name alone. He held no lantern, but his pale, damp face reflected like bone in the moonlight. He looked at the children. He looked at the Void. Finally, he looked at the Creature. "Ah."

"Sir!" Georgie leapt to his feet. "You're here!"

"Is she all right?" the Necromancer asked, facing the Creature.

"I think so," said Georgie. "But she hit her head."

"We'll have to hurry, then." The Necromancer didn't move towards Ellory. Instead, he began circling around the Creature, clicking his tongue in appraisal. "This is rather embarrassing for you, Kaspar. To be captured by such a rudimentary spell?"

The Creature, Kaspar Cynward, moaned in a pained reply.

"You know him?" asked Georgie.

"Well, of course I know him," the Necromancer replied, glancing over his shoulder as he drew a familiar length of chains from his cloak. "It was six, maybe seven, years ago since we met, isn't that right?"

The shackles clinked into place on the Creature's wrists. The Necromancer linked those to the gleaming, metallic collar around Kaspar's neck. With the Necromancer's cloak now spread open, Georgie could see a second twin length of chain and a second collar around the Necromancer's own neck. The shackles around the Necromancer's wrists allowed him more movement, but with a final click and a single length of chain stretched tightly between them, they were chained together.

"My thanks to your father," the Necromancer continued conversationally. "The chain works remarkably well. It even held this thing for far longer than my other methods." He looked at Georgie out of the corner of his eyes. "Until the giant collapsed the tower."

"You said that it couldn't be done," said Georgie. "No Necromancer can resurrect someone from the dead."

The Necromancer snorted, the chains shuddering on his wrists as he gestured towards the Creature. "And they haven't yet. But I am close."

It had been the Necromancer the whole time. *He*'d released the Creature, plucked Kaspar from his final resting place, and had been experimenting with it ever since. As if the Creature were a mere grim plaything and not the mess of tortured bones, mummified flesh, and errant magic before him.

Georgie felt like a fool. The Enchantress's earlier words pierced his heart as swiftly as a lightning strike. *I'm worried his old wounds will lead you on a path too dark for you to follow.*

"You lied," said Georgie. "You lied about everything."

"I did not," said the Necromancer. "I only told you what you were ready to understand. The Fates were not kind to Kaspar. His memory is as torn as his corpse was, but slowly, we've been putting him together." The Necromancer glared at the Creature in front of him. "He has been less than forthcoming with his knowledge, despite my help."

How long had he kept this Creature at bay? Twisting it for his own purposes and creating something that it had never been meant to be? How many had fallen to this Creature? Oldman Woodsman? Georgie's heart thudded with certainty. Or his own mother. Ellory groaned again on the ground behind him. The Creature had almost killed Ellory—and still might if the Necromancer refused to help him.

"You have to release him," said Georgie. "You're hurting people."

"I didn't mean to," the Necromancer replied stiffly. "I've kept it contained as long as I could. These things have a way of...

getting out."

"It's hurting *you*," said Georgie, pointing to the shackles on the Necromancer's wrists.

The Necromancer brushed his concern aside. "I'm fine. Simply keeping my work close is all."

"But you're not!"

The Creature wailed in between them, lurching against its magical binds as Georgie's resolve began to fail. The Necromancer tightened his hold on the chains, yanking the Creature back. "Don't make me angry," warned the Necromancer as the Creature continued to struggle against its bonds. "It won't go well for either of us."

"But why?" pleaded Georgie. "Why are you doing this?"

The Necromancer's face grew very grim. "So no one else has to. I told you before: I will be the last Necromancer. As soon as I can pull every secret and spell from the first. Now, if you would be so kind as to release him."

Georgie bit down on his bottom lip until it bled, fury and sorrow boiling in his chest. He held on to the spell with both hands, the Creature's bones creaking as it tightened around it. "Sir, please. Don't do this."

"You asked me how to bring your mother back," said the Necromancer. "This is how."

"It's not worth it!" Georgie shouted, the magic flaring with a loud crack of lightning.

The Necromancer didn't flinch. "If you will not help me, then I have no further need of you. Your cousin can't wait much longer. Release him. Now."

The Creature caught Georgie's eyes with its mismatched gaze, an empty shell.

With a stifled sob, Georgie released the spell, the magic

dripping off of the Creature like drops of rain. The Creature cried out as if in pain before it fell silent, subdued by the Necromancer's control.

"Lead the way, Kaspar," said the Necromancer.

The Creature shuffled back from Georgie, turning with slow, sodden steps back towards the woods. The Necromancer, bound and chained to his own creation, followed close behind. "Void? Are you coming?"

The cat curled about Georgie's shins. In a surprisingly human motion, she shook her head at the Necromancer.

Her former master stared down at her, clenching his jaw as the Creature reached towards its own heart. A haunted mirror of the Necromancer's own emotions.

"You're leaving me too, then? Giving up on your old friend to save your own skin?"

The Void gave a low, sorrowful mewl.

"Fine," said the Necromancer, even as his own voice cracked. "I'll do this on my own."

With an unforgiving grip, the Necromancer left with the dead, the rattle of silver chains swallowed by the black of night.

Chapter Twenty-Eight

I know not what lies ahead for me now. It may be more striving, more fighting and learning to live with this monster beside me. I do not know how to let go. I don't know if I ever can. But then Morgan appears with a cup of tea and fresh flowers to hide the scent of my undead companion. She believes I can someday be free. Hope feels strange when you are bound to the dead, and yet... I hope she is right.

\- The Dying Art of Necromancy, *T.E.*

* * *

The Void went to fetch help. Georgie stayed by Ellory's side until Callum arrived, anxiously shepherded by the insistent cat on his heels. The young Blacksmith carried Ellory down the mountain while Georgie held tight to his cousin's hand. The Doctor was called and, to the relief of everyone, declared that Ellory would be fine. She would have a wicked headache and would need to take it easy for a few days but would make a full recovery.

Aunt Elisa and the Blacksmith returned the next day. There wasn't much of an explanation that either of the children could offer to dissuade Aunt Elisa's worry. She didn't leave Ellory's side for hours until the Blacksmith, with his solid reassurance, drew her out.

"She wants to speak with you," Aunt Elisa told Georgie.

He found Ellory in bed with a large white bandage wrapped around her forehead. She didn't greet him as he came in. Instead, she stared down at the quilt covering her bed, picking at the loose thread.

"I need to apologize," she said as Georgie sat down next to her. "For everything."

He gave her a reassuring smile. "I'm just glad you're safe."

"Thanks to you," she said. "But it's still my fault that the Necromancer kicked you out."

"How is that your fault?"

"I shouldn't have told you to poke around in his things," Ellory said softly. "Maybe you had your own reasons, but I bullied you into a lot of things you didn't want to do."

But he *had* wanted to do them. He'd wanted to do them so much that he'd almost fallen into the same treacherous canyon that his mentor seemed determined to tread. Alone and hurting, with only the dead to comfort him. Georgie didn't speak, but if not for Ellory, his father, Aunt Elisa, and even the stubborn Void, he might be there with his mentor now.

"I thought that if you learned more about Necromancy, even more than what he wanted you to learn, that you might be able to help me find my da," Ellory continued.

Ellory's father. Of course. Georgie took in the threads all around Ellory's walls. The similarity of their goals, Georgie desperately wanting his mother back while Ellory had searched for her father, made his heart ache.

"Is he dead?" he asked softly.

Ellory shook her head. "I thought he might be. But I told

my mum, and she said he wasn't. She was certain of that much. They don't talk at all, but last she heard, he was living up in Inchante."

The city was a long train ride away, but it was certainly closer than death or the unknown. "Ellory, that's amazing!"

The girl flushed, her eyes lowering in embarrassment. "It is. I can't go to find him yet. Maybe not for a while, but I am sorry that I bullied you. I'm sorry that I didn't listen to you when you told me not to go looking for trouble. You were right."

Georgie grabbed his cousin's hand and gave it a squeeze. "Thanks."

But even in her submissiveness, a touch of Ellory's insatiable curiosity peeked through. "You never did tell me what happened. What did the Necromancer do with Kaspar?"

"I don't know." It was the truth. He hadn't spoken to anyone about what had happened because he was still trying to make sense of it himself. How could he talk about it when it had become apparent that the Necromancer had had a hand in his own mother's death?

Georgie knew he could never tell his father the truth. He didn't need to. His father had already moved on, so Georgie would as well. What was done was done, even if the Necromancer had chained himself to the past.

Ellory deflated a little in disappointment, pressing her lips together so that she wouldn't pry.

Georgie knew what would make her feel better. He pointed up at her head wound. "Callum said that you'll probably have a wicked scar up there."

Ellory's eyes lit up in delight. "Really?"

* * *

In the nights that followed, Georgie often dreamt of the Necromancer, still bound in the chains of his own making. But when he awoke, the Enchantress's scarf would wipe away his tears. He kept it close to him always now, a reminder of gentler magic against the darkness.

Months passed, and the bright leaves of autumn were fading as the winds brought a sharper chill from the mountaintops. Despite the promise of winter, there was a new life to look forward to. Aunt Elisa had yet to say anything, but Georgie had found his father's sketches for a crib in the workshop. Ellory was busy planning her adventure to the city. She was determined to go alone, even if it took a few years of growing up before she could.

Georgie hadn't returned to the Necromancer's cottage since that dreadful night on the cliffside. Not until he was walking home from school, the Void at his heels, and the Enchantress's scarf around his neck led him in a familiar direction.

Here on top of the hill, the Necromancer's cottage looked faded amongst the dying leaves. The tower still lay shattered in ruins upon the ground, and the shutters were closed tight. Only a tendril of smoke from the chimney showed anyone was home at all.

The Enchantress met him on the doorstep.

"Is he inside?" asked Georgie.

The Enchantress's smile wavered with a solemn nod. "He is. Kaspar is still with him."

Georgie's shoulders slumped. "He's never going to let him go, is he?"

"In time, he may," she replied. "But that is up to him."

They walked a little way from the door, towards the well in the courtyard. The Enchantress sat elegantly on the bench beside it, gesturing for Georgie to join her.

"You warned me about him," he said as he sat down. "You were right."

"I wish I hadn't been," she said. "The last time I heard from him was nearly seven years ago. Sardis had just passed and left everything he had to Tristan. I don't know why, but I know it grieved him more than he would dare admit. His time with Sardis had been difficult. I think he wanted his tutor's praise and acceptance. But all he'd left him with were deep scars and a memory that wounded him just as easily. He told me he was going to 'clean out the house and be rid of Necromancy once and for all.' I thought it was a sign that he might finally step out of his tutor's shadow. That he might join me in another magical pursuit." She shook her head. "I did not know that he would go a step further and try to make Necromancy irrelevant or do something so monstrous to prove Sardis wrong."

"He was nice to me," said Georgie. "Or at least, he tried his hardest to be. I didn't always make it very easy for him."

"You are not responsible for his anger and grief, Georgie," said the Enchantress firmly. "That is his burden to bear and his alone. He could have moved on. He could have taken his scars and let go, pursued something else beyond this deep desire to prove to someone he was better. He focused on the imaginary, his own hurt, versus those around him who wanted to help him heal."

Georgie glanced back at the cottage. "But why does he need Kaspar to be the final Necromancer?"

"Necromancy is at its core the desire to eliminate grief," she explained. "Grief has many sources, but most of it circles around death. If there is no more death, there is no more grief. No more scars from those who are lost because we simply never have to lose them.

"I think he thought that if he was more, he'd be happier. He was always looking at what he didn't have instead of what was in front of him. In the end, it's ironic, really. He went searching for more power and ended up doing what no one else has done for centuries. He already has it, but he convinced himself that he needed more."

Georgie understood that with remarkable clarity. He'd thought that he'd needed his mother to make his family whole, and he'd nearly missed the fact that it had been for a long time.

"I won't speak anymore for him," she said. "But what he is going through is as tangled as the chains he keeps around that creature."

"What can I do?" he asked.

The Enchantress placed her hand gently on his cheek. "Oh, Georgie. There is nothing you can do. This is not your responsibility."

"But is he yours?"

The Enchantress thought for a moment. "It is the responsibility I have chosen," she said slowly. "For now. I'm an adult. I get to do that. But I promise you, he won't be alone with his monster or his grief. Not anymore."

Georgie nodded. "Well, if you're going to take care of him, you should know that he doesn't take two sugars in his tea anymore. He hates wet socks but forgets to leave them near the fire to dry, and he really needs to clean out the closet so that Herbert has more room."

The Enchantress smiled at each instruction. Her hand still rested on his shoulder, her fingers lingering around the scarf on his neck. "Here," she said, murmuring a spell beneath her breath. The scarf tingled and fluttered about Georgie's neck, settling into an emerald-green color. "This ought to suit you better."

"Thank you," said Georgie. "For everything."

"You're very welcome. And if you should ever need me..." She tapped the edge of the scarf before letting go. "This will help."

There was a quiet meow at Georgie's feet. The Void stared at the doorway to the Necromancer's house, her tail flicking back and forth with indecision.

"You can go if you want to," said Georgie, surprised at how lonely that made him.

The Void looked up at the Enchantress, and to the surprise of them both, she hopped up into the woman's lap.

The Enchantress stayed still, listening to something unheard as the Void held her gaze for a long moment. Then, ever so slowly, the Void blinked. The cat butted her head into the Enchantress's open palm once, twice, and then a third time before she leapt down and returned to Georgie's side.

"What just happened?" asked Georgie.

The Enchantress was just as incredulous. "She's decided to stay with you."

The Void chirped back in agreement, wrapping herself around Georgie's ankles. Georgie scooped up the Void from the ground. The cat let him, purring against his chest with unnatural adoration. "Yoricsgrave will still need a Necromancer," the Enchantress said thoughtfully. "But perhaps a different kind. It is a decision you alone can make."

Georgie wondered what it would look like to follow the Necromancer's intentions versus his path. He could guard the dead, keeping those who would seek to disturb their rest at bay. The mourning would need comfort, a caretaker, and he was good at that. There was a lot of hope left for the living. The Necromancer may not have wanted it now, but perhaps someday, he would.

The Enchantress seemed to sense his thoughts. "I think you've seen more than enough of death for a while, Georgie. Go and live."

THE END

Acknowledgments

Writing is a solitary pursuit, but books are published because of community. I'm so blessed to have so many lovely bookish folk in my corner.

Thank you to Snowy Wings Publishing and Lyssa for taking me literally beneath their wings. I'm so thrilled to have been connected and to have such great champions for my stories.

Many thanks to my copy editor Amy McNulty, and my Proofreader, Irene S. from Red Adept Publishing for fixing all of my commas.

Thanks to Matilda Sevón, my translator for the Necromancer's Finnish spells. You went above and beyond to find the proper words and are infinitely superior to Google Translate.

Shout out to my wonderful cover artist, Luisa Galstyan. Your work is exceptional!

My mentor, Laura E. Weymouth, my beloved Baba Yaga. I'm so grateful for your insight, generosity, and all the endless doors you've opened for me. You're the best.

To my early readers: Brooke Findley, I'm so glad we connected and I can't wait for the world to see your stories. Cara Dyne-Gores, you are still my favorite bookseller. Kelsi Johnson, thank you for your enthusiasm and beautiful artwork! Marie Farb and Family, I'm honored that you read this together. Thank you for your notes and laughter!

To Meg Caddy. You were the first to read my work and still

say nice things about the truly terrible drafts I've sent you for over ten years now. I promise to save my best puns for you.

Many thanks to my indie publishing fairy godmothers: Wendee Gingell, Suzannah Rowntree, Intisar Khanani, and Claire Trella Hill. I could not have done this without you. Thank you for answering questions graciously, encouraging me to Do the Thing, and providing resources beyond my wildest imagination.

To my co-workers and friends at 082, truly the best store. Thank you for putting up with all my whimsy.

To the Wayward Tokens: Bee, Dave, Jake and Violeta. I love all of our adventures together. Here's to many, many more!

To my TBD Party: Ani, Bekah, Claire and V(again), I promise I won't murder you. Please pick an actual name for the group.

To The Thing with Feathers: Y'all are truly a godsend in every sense of the word. Thank you for your prayers, encouragement, laughter and companionship. I adore you.

Thanks to my family, for taking me to the library and letting me bring home armfuls of books every week. And a special thanks to my niece and nephews for reminding me how precious childhood is and just how magnificently clever kids can be.

Many thanks to my friends, Rachel Lewis, Michelle Ianellio, Tina Riedy, Shawna Howson, Tabi Berkey, Liz Vallish Adams, Brianna Barton, Erin Hill, and many others.

To The #WritingCommunity of Twitter. I literally learned everything about publishing from you. To everyone whose hosted pitch events, shared their experiences, taught through threads, and cheered me on. This is for you.

About the Author

Beverly Twomey was born and raised in Cincinnati, Ohio. For over ten years, she has worked as a used bookseller which has greatly expanded her personal Tolkien collection. When she is not lost in the stacks, she can be found drinking vast amounts of tea, snuggling with her two cats, reading fantasy novels, writing in the wee hours of the morning and plotting ways to play more Dungeons and Dragons.

You can connect with me on:
- http://bevtwomey.wordpress.com
- https://twitter.com/BevTwomey
- https://www.facebook.com/bevwritesbooks
- https://www.instagram.com/eomira

Subscribe to my newsletter:
- https://gnomeandcats.substack.com

www.ingramcontent.com/pod-product-compliance
Lightning Source LLC
Chambersburg PA
CBHW030749190726
48285CB00003B/772